blemos

D1461983

SPECIAL MESSAGE TO READERS

THE ULVERSCROFT FOUNDATION
(registered UK charity number 264873)
was established in 1972 to provide funds for
research, diagnosis and treatment of eye diseases.
Examples of major projects funded by
the Ulverscroft Foundation are:-

- The Children's Eye Unit at Moorfields Eye Hospital, London
- The Ulverscroft Children's Eye Unit at Great Ormond Street Hospital for Sick Children
- Funding research into eye diseases and treatment at the Department of Ophthalmology, University of Leicester
- The Ulverscroft Vision Research Group, Institute of Child Health
- Twin operating theatres at the Western Ophthalmic Hospital, London
- The Chair of Ophthalmology at the Royal Australian College of Ophthalmologists

You can help further the work of the Foundation
by making a donation or leaving a legacy.
Every contribution is gratefully received. If you
would like to help support the Foundation or
require further information, please contact:

THE ULVERSCROFT FOUNDATION
The Green, Bradgate Road, Anstey
Leicester LE7 7FU, England
Tel: (0116) 236 4325

website: www.ulverscroft-foundation.org.uk

MEDITERRANEAN MYSTERY

Leda unexpectedly finds herself companion to her great aunt on a Mediterranean cruise. Assuming it will be a boring holiday with a crowd of elderly people, her horizons change as she explores the ports of call, and discovers that Aunt Ronnie is lively company. There's also a handsome ship's officer who seems to be attracted to Leda, plus intriguing fellow passenger Nick, who's hiding something. Added into the mix is a mystery on the ship — which becomes a voyage with unforeseen consequences . . .

EVELYN ORANGE

◆

MEDITERRANEAN MYSTERY

Complete and Unabridged

LINFORD
Leicester

First published in Great Britain in 2019

First Linford Edition
published 2020

Copyright © 2019 by DC Thomson & Co. Ltd.,
and Evelyn Orange
All rights reserved

A catalogue record for this book is available
from the British Library.

ISBN 978–1–4448–4527–3

Published by
Ulverscroft Limited
Anstey, Leicestershire

Set by Words & Graphics Ltd.
Anstey, Leicestershire
Printed and bound in Great Britain by
T. J. International Ltd., Padstow, Cornwall

This book is printed on acid-free paper

1

Taking Aunt Ronnie's arm, Leda obediently turned a bright expression to the photographer. She hoped her smile would give the impression she was enthusiastic about boarding a cruise ship, even though she didn't feel it.

Behind them stretched a queue of travellers excitedly chatting in the entrance hall to the docks. There was a flash from the camera, and the photographer waved them on with a cheery grin. Immediately his attention switched to the next people to be snapped.

'I'm so pleased you could come with me, Leda,' Aunt Ronnie said as she tapped her walking stick along beside her. They were heading to the transport bus that would take them to the ship. 'When your mother broke her wrist, I thought it would be the end of my trip.

I don't know if I'll manage another one. I'm really getting too old.'

Already the heat of Palma, capital of the Mediterranean island of Majorca, was penetrating to the two women, freshly arrived from England. May in England had been showery and cool, but it was more like high summer here. Leda wiped her forehead with her free arm, feeling overdressed in the jeans and jacket she'd chosen for travelling.

'Nonsense! You'll be back again next year, just you see,' she said, resolving to enjoy the Mediterranean heat, and the company of her mother's Aunt Veronica. At eighty-three, Aunt Ronnie was a real sweetie, marvellous for her years. Her brain was sharp as a pin, and though she was troubled by arthritis, on the whole she was doing very well.

It was only a week ago that Leda's mother had phoned her.

'Leda, you'll have to go with Aunt Ronnie on the cruise. I was playing tennis yesterday when I fell badly and broke my wrist. I'm all strapped up, and the doctors say I'd be very unwise to travel next week.'

'Mum! You can't expect me to drop everything and go on holiday. I have a business to run!'

'You're free next week, aren't you? I thought you said that your last job had finished and you had nothing until June. A little holiday will be just the thing for you — and it's all paid for.'

Not my idea of a holiday, Leda had thought grimly. Looking after an old lady on a cruise with a whole lot of other geriatrics! Then she chided herself. That wasn't fair. Aunt Ronnie was a dear, and it was true, she had just finished her last commission, and there were another three weeks before she started her next job.

Leda had gone freelance as an interior stylist eight months ago. Everyone had thrown up their hands when she told them what she planned, saying it was totally the wrong time to be starting her own business. But she'd had several requests for private work,

3

which had given her six months of commissions and started her off well. The satisfied clients had spread the word, and there were regular jobs coming in now. It looked as if the business was going to be a success.

Maybe a holiday would be a good idea, giving her a total break after the frenzy and uncertainty of the past months — even if it wasn't the sort of vacation she would have chosen for herself.

Now, with the Majorcan sun beating down on her head, she helped Aunt Ronnie off the bus which had taken them down the quay. They gazed up at the impressive expanse of white ship docked at the quayside. It did look very enticing, with all the people in holiday clothes laughing excitedly as they were boarding.

Maybe it wouldn't be so bad after all, Leda thought. The ship would be calling at some famous ports in the Mediterranean that Leda had always thought would be interesting to visit.

She could put up with the dinners and the cocktails and afternoon teas. A few good books, her MP3 and some sunbathing would help her get through.

Two smart crew members, a man and a woman dressed in white with navy blue and gold epaulettes on their shoulders, smiled and welcomed them on board as they reached the top of the little gangplank.

'Welcome to the Crime Writing Cruise on the Ocean Star!' the woman said.

Leda turned to Aunt Ronnie in dismay.

'Crime writing? What's all this about? Mum never said there was a theme to the cruise.'

Aunt Ronnie chuckled mischievously.

'You've found out my little secret. I've always enjoyed crime novels, and though I don't want to write myself, I'm going to have fun attending all these lectures and workshops. You might even try it yourself, dear.'

A look of horror crossed Leda's face. 'Not me!'

They offered their new ship's identity cards to be scanned and stepped on board the vessel that would be their home for the next seven days.

The interior of the ship was pleasantly cool after being out in the fierce sun. A tall, black-haired male officer with tanned features and a wide smile greeted everyone as they entered. His high cheekbones and sculpted good looks were set off admirably by his white uniform.

'Now, that's what I call tasty,' Ronnie murmured out of the side of her mouth.

Leda giggled. 'Auntie! You'll get us thrown into the brig with talk like that!'

Ronnie turned twinkling eyes up at her. 'You don't find a man in uniform attractive?'

Leda managed to compose herself before they reached the officer. He was taller than Leda by a good few inches, which she always found gratifying. Being five foot eleven, not many men were taller than her, but it made her feel more feminine. He welcomed them both aboard, then gazed deep into Leda's eyes, smiling slowly. The irises of his eyes were almost black, fringed by long dark lashes that she envied.

'My name is Iannis, and I am Second Officer of the Ocean Star,' he introduced himself. 'Any problems with your cruise, you must come to me. Dear ladies, what are your names?'

Almost mesmerised by his gaze, Leda introduced her great aunt, then herself. She just couldn't stop staring! What was wrong with her?

'Now, here is Andras.' He waved a hand towards a crew member beaming at them, wearing a deep red jacket over a white shirt and black trousers. 'He will show you to your cabin. Enjoy your cruise.'

With a little shake of her shoulders, Leda broke their eye contact, murmuring, 'Thank you.'

Ronnie was already showing her security card displaying the cabin number to Andras, who glanced at it and immediately headed to the lifts.

He left them at the door of their cabin with a cheery wave, wishing them a happy cruise.

They had been informed earlier that their luggage would arrive within the hour. The cabin was quite small, but Leda was relieved to discover they had a porthole. Either side of it were two single beds, reached by passing a tiny shower room, opposite a neat built-in wardrobe and dressing table. Above this was a mirror that covered the wall up to the ceiling, and tucked beneath it were two padded stools.

Ronnie threw her handbag and jacket on to the bed on the same side as the shower room, then sat on it, kicking off her shoes. 'Since we can't do any unpacking yet, I think I'll put my feet up for a while and maybe have a little snooze.'

Leda took both of their jackets and hung them up in the wardrobe.

'Good idea. If you don't mind, I think I'll do some exploring to orientate myself. If this is to be our gilded cage for the next week, I want to find out where everything is.'

* * *

Leaving the cabin with just her key card in the pocket of her jeans, Leda looked round each deck inside the ship, locating the two restaurants, the spa and gym, the show theatre, several bars with dance or activity areas, and a cocktail lounge that was already filling up with guests.

She noted the location of the information desk, the excursion booth, and finally worked her way up the open decks in turn. Some people had already bagged sunbeds and were exposing their pale British limbs to the sun. No doubt they wouldn't remain milky white for long!

Leda wondered whether to buy a cool drink, as all she needed to do was swipe her cabin card. But she spied a small swimming pool with deliciously inviting blue water. So instead she decided to nip back down to the cabin to see if the luggage had arrived so she could find her swimming costume.

Aunt Ronnie was awake when she opened the door, and their two suitcases were now sitting beside the bed.

'They just arrived. Would you be a dear and lift mine on to my bed so I can do some unpacking?'

Leda did so, and as they quickly put their clothes in the wardrobe and drawers, she explained what she had seen on her walk, and that she fancied a swim.

'I'll come with you,' Ronnie said, as Leda tucked the suitcases into the end of the wardrobe. 'I could do with a cup of tea.'

It didn't take Leda long to change, so they made their way up to the pool deck.

Ronnie exclaimed with delight at the view from the deck over the harbour teeming with yachts, their white masts dipping and bobbing in the warm breeze. The sweep of the bay led their gaze to the pale gothic shape of Palma Cathedral. She lifted her face up to the sun, beating down from a clear blue sky.

'This is what I've been looking forward to.'

With her great aunt safely ensconced at one of the little tables, and an attentive waiter at her side, Leda slipped off her tunic, revealing a sleek black swimsuit.

'Didn't you get yourself something more holiday-like?' Aunt Ronnie said, putting her sunglasses on.

Leda shook her head. 'I swim at my local leisure centre twice a week, and this is one of my costumes. If I wore a tropical outfit, or a bikini, the other serious swimmers would laugh me out of the pool.' She picked up the towel supplied in their cabin and walked over to the ship's pool.

The blue water, slightly ruffled by the breeze, looked cool and refreshing.

Surprised that no one else was swimming already, she stepped on to the tiles at the side of the pool and slipped into the water. Immediately she gave a gasp of shock as the icy cold water knocked the breath out of her. She had expected the water to be as warm as the air around her, not registering that the pool was in the shade — and would have been for several hours.

A deep laugh sounded above her, making her look up sharply. She dashed a lock of long, dark, wet hair out of her eyes.

'What's so funny?' she snapped at the owner of the laugh, trying to stop herself from shivering.

'Sorry, it was the look of shock on your face. I couldn't help myself.'

A long, lean male figure stood by the pool, holding a glass containing some colourful drink topped with a tiny blue umbrella. Leda tried to ignore the strong, athletic legs that emerged from his shorts, the toned chest that was clearly visible through his open-necked shirt. A curl of unruly brown hair fell over one eye, the other twinkling as he surveyed her in her watery surroundings.

'Well, you can just go away and leave me to have my swim in peace.'

So saying, she launched herself into a swift crawl, hoping that she could produce an impressive style before the feeling went out of her arms and legs altogether. No way was she chickening out with this man laughing at her. It didn't take long to reach the other side of the small pool, but she turned immediately and forged her way back again. No wonder the pool was empty, she thought as she bravely ploughed up and down, trying to ignore the growing numbness in her body. Eventually she decided enough was enough, and she had upheld her dignity by not getting out immediately. Quickly scanning the immediate area, there was no sign of the annoying man, so she decided it was safe to emerge from the water.

Throwing her towel over her shoulders, she saw her tormentor sitting chatting to Aunt Ronnie, filling the only other seat at the table. Furious, she stalked over to confront him.

'Leda, dear, this kind young man has kept me company while you were exercising.'

Aunt Ronnie was clearly charmed, but Leda was determined not to be. She didn't like being mocked, especially by an attractive man. It held too many bad memories for her.

The intruder stood up and she was surprised to find that he was several inches taller than her. Remembering the officer who welcomed them on board, she registered that it wasn't often she met two men who topped her in height within such a short span of time.

'Nicholas Drake, pleased to meet you.'

A little shiver passed over her, and she wasn't sure if it was because she was cold from her swim, or the

14

nearness of this man. Or maybe it was her hackles rising? No, she would not be won over by charm.

She spoke coolly. 'Leda Hollings. I see you've already met Aunt Veronica.'

'Ronnie, please! Only my parents called me Veronica. It's so old-fashioned, I soon changed it.' She chuckled, giving an impression of the attractive young woman she had once been. 'My dear departed husband, Bill, used to say I was only Veronica when I wanted to apply for a job or run a committee!'

Leda smiled at her great aunt, but then turned an icy glance at Nicholas Drake. 'Well, Mr Drake, I'm back, so I can look after Aunt Ronnie now.'

He lifted his glass, nearly empty. 'I was hoping I could tempt you with a drink to celebrate the start of the cruise. And please, call me Nick. Like your aunt, I'm only Nicholas on formal occasions.'

'I'm sorry, I really need to change out of my wet swimming costume. Do you want to stay here, Aunt Ronnie?'

Sensing the tension, Ronnie shook her head. 'I've had my tea, dear, and I think we should finish unpacking. We need to change for dinner, as well. I'd like to go to the early sitting.'

'Well, maybe I'll see you ladies later.' Nick Drake finished his drink and left the glass on the table, waving to them amicably as he left them.

Leda didn't speak to Ronnie until they had passed the bar and were inside the ship again. She resisted the temptation to look back to the deck and see which direction he had taken.

'What an insufferable man! Fancy pushing himself in to sit beside you like that.'

Ronnie gave a little smile.

'I can see he ruffled your feathers, dear, but he was absolutely charming with me. I enjoyed his company. I like meeting friendly people. Don't be so harsh.'

The lift arrived, and they entered, the doors closing behind them.

'I just don't like pushy people, Auntie. Did you hear him laughing at me when I went in the pool?'

'You're a little wound up still, and not quite in a holiday mood yet. Why not just relax and enjoy the cruise? I think we should go to the talk tomorrow, about the places we're visiting. Then we can decide what excursions we want to book. It's all very exciting, seeing these famous places. Fancy me getting to see them for the first time at my age — I thought I never would.'

Her mood brightening, Leda decided to put the annoying Nick Drake out of her mind. He was probably some type of professional who fancied himself as a crime writer, and scribbled drivel in his spare time! Well, he could mingle with all the other sad people who imagined themselves to be undiscovered best-selling authors. Leda would simply enjoy the sun and the relaxation.

2

The cabin was pleasantly cool, with a view from the porthole of yachts anchored in the bay at Palma. As Leda laid the cabin keycard on the dressing table, she noticed a white envelope that she hadn't seen before. On the front was scrawled a large capital L, underlined firmly. Turning it over, she noticed it was sealed.

She showed it to Ronnie. 'Auntie, was this here before we left the cabin?'

Ronnie was sitting on her bed, unfastening her sandals. 'No, I don't remember seeing that before I left. It seems to be addressed to you. Why don't you open it?'

Leda tore it open. Inside was a single sheet of paper with a message printed on it: *Meet me at 2230 tonight on Deck 9 outside the Spa.*

There was no signature. Frowning,

Leda turned it over, but the back was blank. She handed the letter to Ronnie.

'Will you go?'

'Would it be safe?'

Ronnie raised her eyebrows. 'Well, this is intriguing. If you don't go, you'll forever wonder who sent you a mysterious note. You must have a secret admirer!'

'Auntie, you have a very vivid imagination!' Leda sat on the bed beside her. 'I don't suppose any harm would come of it. After all, it should be safe on board ship. There are bound to be other people around.'

Ronnie gave a roguish smile. 'I could always come with you.'

Leda laughed. 'No, I'll go alone — if I go. We'll see. I'll make up my mind later.' She put the note back in its envelope and on the dressing table against the mirror.

After half an hour of relaxing, they looked out a change of clothes to wear to their first dinner on board ship.

'Leda, what do you think? Too

dressed-up?' Ronnie asked, handing Leda her pearl necklace so she could fasten the clasp at the back of her aunt's neck.

'Nonsense — you look just right. If we're going to the formal dining room, we want to look smart. Then they'll seat us with someone respectable!'

Leda wore a pair of wide black trousers with a white embroidered tunic top, with gold dangly earrings and matching necklace. 'Will I do?'

'Of course. And remember to sparkle, dear. You get too lost in your own thoughts sometimes. Try to relax. You might meet a dishy man. It's been too long since you had someone in your life.'

'Aunt Ronnie, you promised you wouldn't try matchmaking. I may be twenty-nine, but it's not like it was in your day. I don't define myself by getting married. I have a business to run.'

Why did everyone think she needed romance in her life? The last one had been a disaster, and she was happier on her own.

As they left the cabin, pulling the door locked behind them, her great aunt shook her head. 'Yes, but you still need a special person. It's a year since you broke up with your last boyfriend.'

Leda shuddered. 'A year last month, and don't remind me. I'm so much happier since I split with Damien. He tried to control everything, until I felt I'd lost my own personality. I'm not going to let that happen again.'

'You lost your confidence when you were with him, but not all men are like Damien. That was a nice young man we were speaking to this afternoon by the pool . . . '

'Auntie . . . ' Leda said, wagging her finger at her in mock warning. They laughed as they stepped into the lift.

At the entrance to the Ocean Suite dining room, the head waiter, dressed formally in a black suit, asked them their cabin number and allocated them places at a table for four by the window.

21

The other two seats were currently vacant. He helped Aunt Ronnie with her chair, balancing her stick so it wouldn't fall while she was eating.

Leda looked round the restaurant and was surprised at how many younger people there were on the cruise. Her idea that it would be all elderly voyagers was proving to be completely wrong.

She had just started reading the menu when she was aware of a commotion at a table in the centre of the restaurant. A couple, similar in age to her, were arguing with the maitre d' before they stalked over towards Leda and Ronnie's table.

'I'm sorry to trouble you, but would you mind if my wife and I join you ladies? She's set her heart on a window table, and the head waiter has agreed to let us change.'

Leda laid down her menu in astonishment, aware that another older couple were being herded away as they approached the table, and directed to the places that had just been vacated. She caught sight of them looking with bewildered expressions across to the window table.

Aware that Ronnie was greeting the newcomers politely, she tore her gaze away from the others and met the eyes of the man who had joined them. He pulled out the chair opposite her and sat down, while his wife slid into the seat across from her great aunt.

'Let me introduce myself — I'm Jason Rundle, and this is my wife, Tish.'

He was of average height, with light brown hair that curled over the collar of his shirt. He had dressed for the evening in a dark blue linen jacket and shirt with a blue tie with green and yellow palm trees. Leda supposed it must be his holiday tie, and wondered if his wife had chosen it.

Jason shook Aunt Ronnie's hand gently, then took Leda's, but seemed to hold on to it longer than was necessary. With a little shiver, she pulled it away quickly.

He shook out his serviette immediately and placed it on his lap, then turned to Ronnie. 'And where have you travelled from? We're from Peterborough.'

Ronnie smiled politely. 'I'm from Durham, and my great niece lives in Newcastle-upon-Tyne.'

'Oh, that's a lovely part of the world,' Tish Rundle said in a high voice, her sentence ending in a giggle. 'We went there for a weekend last year, and really enjoyed it, didn't we, darling?' She rubbed her hand over her husband's arm, looking at him with fawning eyes, which were heavily made up with false eyelashes. Then she turned to Leda, smiling with bright, even teeth. 'This is so lovely. I absolutely adore the glamour of a cruise. The wonderful food, the service, exotic cocktails, and endless entertainment. We've cruised twice before. How about you?'

Leda shook her head. 'This is our first. Aunt Ronnie always wanted to come on a cruise, and was to have been

24

with my mother, but she broke her wrist last week, so I stepped in.'

'Then we're very lucky to have your company.' Jason Rundle's words were innocuous, but there was something in his gaze that made Leda feel slightly uncomfortable. He just seemed to look into her eyes for too long. She was glad when their waiter arrived to take their choices for the meal. Once he had disappeared, Jason turned to her intently. 'So, what do you do in Durham?'

'Newcastle. I'm an interior designer — I run my own business.'

'How marvellous!' Tish's squeaky voice shrilled out, making the diners at the next table turn their heads. 'That must be such an exciting job, don't you agree, darling?' She grabbed her husband's hand with both of hers, and pulled it to her chest, gazing into his eyes.

Astonished at this reaction, Leda didn't dare look at Ronnie in case she burst out laughing!

25

Jason turned to her with a bright smile.

'We're very humdrum in comparison, just office workers. This is our escape to glamour for a few days each year!' He gave a hearty laugh, which was interrupted by the wine waiter bringing the bottle of wine the Rundles had chosen.

While Jason made a great fuss of tasting it and then passing the glass to his wife, Leda risked a glance at Ronnie. Her great aunt raised her eyebrows slightly, which made her realise they would have a lot to say about their dinner companions when they returned to their cabin.

Conversation flowed quite easily, despite her feeling of unease. Leda wasn't quite sure what it was about the couple that seemed odd. They acted as if they were very much in love, but surely she wasn't mistaken in the way his eyes raked her every now and then. Plus there was that odd scene earlier when they changed tables.

26

The meal was excellent, even though she found the company distracting. Despite her vow to forget her earlier encounter, she found her eyes straying round the crowded dining room, searching for a tall figure with brown hair. How ridiculous! She didn't even want to speak to Nicholas Drake again, so why was she looking for him? She would do better to search for that handsome Greek officer with the gorgeous eyes. A touch of romance — with no strings — would be just the ticket, Aunt Ronnie would say.

The ship was due to leave port at half past nine that evening. While they were dining, an announcement from the Entertainments Manager over the loud-speaker informed them there would be a party until the small hours on deck to celebrate the start of the cruise.

Tish's voice was shrill with excitement.

'We must go to that! It's always such fun — the entertainment group per-form live, and I believe some of the crew are performing as a rock band. Are you coming?'

'I'm not sure — I don't know if it will suit Aunt Ronnie.' Leda didn't fancy joining a drunken knees-up, and looked at her great aunt, hoping she would decline. In any case, she had her mysterious rendezvous at half past ten.

To her surprise, Ronnie was in the mood for something new. 'I think we should show our faces and I want to see the ship leave port, as it's my first cruise.' Ronnie beamed at them all. 'Maybe we'll see you up on deck. But I think I'd better go and have a little rest before all the excitement.'

As they walked back to their cabin, Ronnie took Leda's arm.

'I could tell you didn't want to go, dear, but you really must unbend a little. You've been stuck in your ivory tower for too long.'

'Aunt Ronnie, you've no idea what these things are like . . . wild dancing, drinking, shouting . . . '

'Sounds like fun — and just what you

need. You can park me in a chair, and I'll enjoy watching all you young people enjoying yourselves.'

'But what about the note about the meeting?' Leda began to wonder if she should just ignore it, but her curiosity was still aroused.

Ronnie patted her hand. 'I haven't forgotten that. You can walk me back to the cabin at twenty past ten, and then you'll have time to meet your mystery admirer.'

3

They made their way up to the boat deck half an hour before the ship was due to leave port. Aunt Ronnie had persuaded Leda to wear something more partyish, so she had changed into a short white dress with gold sandals. An older man kindly vacated a chair near the rail so Aunt Ronnie could see the deck below and the lights of the port as they left.

A canopy had been erected beside the swimming pool, beneath which a rock group of five members — two men on guitars, a drummer, a woman on keyboards, and a female singer — was in full flow. Leda had to admit they were rather good. Around the pool, members of the entertainment group were dancing and singing to the music the group played, clapping their hands and encouraging people around them to join in. Everyone looked as if they were having a good time, and soon Leda found it impossible not to tap her feet and sway in time to the music. Aunt Ronnie beamed, clapping even though the music was way more modern than she was used to.

Then the ship's hooter gave several great toots, making them all clap their hands over their ears, laughing. As the sound dissipated into the warm air, the entertainments manager, Craig, shouted, 'The Ocean Star has now set sail. Happy cruising, everyone!'

The passengers responded with an ear-splitting cheer. The band began another number, and several people got up to dance. The lights of Palma began to move as the ship drew away from the quay.

'Amazing, isn't it? Don't you fancy joining in?'

Her heart leapt in her chest at the deep voice next to her, familiar even over the loud music and laughter of the party on the deck below.

Faking a cool demeanour, she turned to face Nick Drake, willing herself not to be won over by the easy smile. 'I don't see you joining in either.'

He folded his arms on the rail, his elbow almost touching hers. The nearness of him made her pulse skip. Foolish girl! She was acting as if she had never been near a man before. And such an annoying one, as well! She edged away slightly, so her elbow wouldn't be close enough to make contact with his. She had a feeling his touch would send an electric shock through her.

'I'm no dancer,' he said, oblivious of the emotions warring inside her. 'But I do like music, and it's amusing to watch other people having a good. time. I would have thought you would be good at that sort of thing.' His eyes took in her body, fit from her swimming and exercise. Somehow his glance didn't give her the creepy feeling she had experienced earlier with Jason — instead it made her want to shiver with pleasure, a sensation she tried to ignore.

She swung away from him. 'No, I'm not fond of cavorting around in front of other people.'

His eyes narrowed. 'You don't like being watched?'

Her eyes flashed in response. 'I don't like being judged.'

Unpleasant memories of her last relationship flashed into her mind. It was almost two years before she had realised how much Damien had undermined her confidence. It had taken her another six months to break with him, as she was always trying to live up to his vision of what she should be. Only now was she beginning to feel comfortable in her own skin again. She felt fit and healthy, exercising regularly, and the successes she had scored in her new business boosted her confidence. No way was she going to let another man intrude on that feeling of wellbeing.

Still, she shouldn't be rude to this stranger who was clearly trying to be friendly. Leda looked up at him, enjoying the fact that he was taller than her. That was another niggle with Damien — he had been the same height as her, so hated her wearing heels, saying she looked unfeminine towering over him. Now it was great to wear fabulous shoes whenever she wanted. It occurred to her that Nick was tall enough for her to wear any of the heels in her wardrobe. She couldn't stop a little smile tugging at her lips at the thought.

His eyes crinkled with pleasure. 'That's an expression I haven't seen on your face before. What brought that on?'

Suddenly feeling as if her private thoughts were exposed, she turned away. 'Nothing. It's the atmosphere, I suppose.' Her voice was breathless, trying to hide the truth, that he was penetrating her shell. 'I must see if Aunt Ronnie would like a drink.'

Ronnie was tapping her hand on the table in time to the music, enjoying the spectacle below. 'I'm perfectly all right, dear,' she insisted when Leda asked her about a drink. 'You should go off and enjoy yourself with young Nick.'

'No, Auntie, I'm here with you.'

She felt a stab of panic, and wasn't entirely sure why. She wasn't ready to get involved with a man — least of all this annoying one, she thought fiercely. Glancing back to the rail, she saw him looking down at the dancers, and pushed to one side the slight regret that she needed to slip away for that rendezvous. She could just stay — but if she did, she'd never find out who'd sent the note.

'How long do you want to stay, Auntie?'

Ronnie glanced at her watch and nodded. 'You're right, I shouldn't stay up too late. It's been a long day, with all the travelling, and I feel tired.' She reached for her stick and struggled to her feet. 'Will you say goodnight to Nick?'

Leda took her arm. 'No, I'm not going to risk him seeing us back to the cabin. I'll need to get away smartly to be in time for my . . . meeting.'

She didn't want to have to explain herself to Nick. It was just a bit of fun, really, to see who would send her such a message. Nothing could happen on the ship . . . could it?

★　★　★

They were out of sight before Nick realised they were gone. As the time approached to meet this unknown person, Leda was beginning to feel nervous. Maybe she should just go to bed as well — it had been a long day with all the travelling.

But Ronnie told her to comb her hair and hurry off. She showed Leda the new book she was keen to start reading. 'I've brought the new Harry Agnew novel with me, as he's the keynote speaker on the last evening. I want him to sign my copy, but I intend to enjoy it first.' She laid it down and tapped her wristwatch. 'Now, you'd better be off, or you'll be late. If I'm asleep when you get back, you can tell me all about it in the morning.'

Leda grabbed a cardigan to keep the chill from her shoulders and slipped out into the corridor.

Further down the corridor a middle-aged couple entered their cabin, but apart from that it was deserted. The sound of party music drifted faintly down the stairwells. A woman crew member in a black skirt and white blouse with black epaulettes passed Leda as she made her way upstairs.

Leda was barely out of breath when she reached Deck 9. She remembered seeing the spa at the opposite end of the ship earlier, and wended her way down the corridor on the port side of the ship. A woman passenger carrying a cerise-coloured wrap emerged from a cabin as she passed, and greeted her with a pleasant 'Good evening' before setting off to the stairs and lifts. While the cabin door was open, Leda caught a glimpse of a luxurious double bed, a table with two chairs, and a full-length window that no doubt led to a balcony.

For a moment she fantasised about spending her cruise in such an up-market cabin, compared with the tiny accommodation she and Ronnie were in. Well, at least they had a porthole! Besides, she was sure they wouldn't be spending much time in the cabin, as there was plenty to do on the ship even when they weren't in port.

These thoughts occupied her until she reached the end of the corridor, and stood outside the full-length glass panels of the ship's spa. It was decorated with swirls of blue and turquoise in a representation of waves, scattered with coral-coloured starfish and dark blue fish shapes. A sign outside declared it was closed, and listed the opening times. On the inside of the glass was a schedule of all the treatments available.

Glancing at her watch she realised she was still a few minutes early. Leda began to read through the spa treatments to keep her mind occupied.

Several minutes passed. Each move and creak of the ship or the doors made her look up with expectation. The faint sound of music and laughter from the party on deck filtered through. She wondered if Nick Drake was still at the party, and what he'd thought when they'd left. Had he missed her? *Stop it!* she told herself sternly, and returned to wondering who had sent the message.

As more time passed, she remained alone. The tension of anticipation had dissipated, and instead a mixture of irritation and disappointment began to wash over her. How long should she wait? It was already ten to eleven.

Then her eyes caught a movement beyond the door marked Crew Only to the left of the spa. Through the frosted glass she could discern the shapes of two people. One was tall enough to be a man, and she could tell he was wearing white. The other, in dark clothes, could have been a woman, but she couldn't make out any details. Then the door opened and the man emerged. Of the other person there was no sign.

When Leda recognised the crew member who had introduced himself as the Second Officer, her heart began to hammer, though she wasn't sure whether from pleasure or embarrassment. Iannis stepped out confidently, but hesitated when he saw her standing there.

'Good evening? Are you all right?' A small frown appeared on his forehead.

Her heart sank a little. It seemed this was not the person she was here to meet.

'Yes, thank you. I was just . . . just looking at the treatments in the spa. I may treat myself.'

'You're Leda, are you not?' He gave her a devastatingly attractive smile.

Had he remembered her from the introduction when they came on board, or had he indeed sent her the note? Emotions warred within her. 'Yes.'

'Are you not interested in the party

on deck? It is always very entertaining.'

Thinking quickly, she said, 'It's a bit loud for me. I prefer my entertainment more subtle.'

He came to stand more closely, and she was aware of his dark eyes gazing intently at her. At this distance she caught a faint scent of some tangy aftershave, and at that moment she felt a tug of attraction. There was a slight pause before he continued, a pause that made her hold her breath in anticipation.

'It would be my pleasure to entertain such an attractive young lady. I am on duty until midnight tonight. Would you care to join me for a drink when I am free?' His white teeth flashed.

Leda was torn. He was incredibly handsome. Wouldn't it be pleasant to indulge in a little flirtation? Or should she wait to see if anyone else turned up? Something made her keep quiet about receiving a note, as he hadn't mentioned it. Finally she shook her head, deciding this was not the time to be having a drink with a stranger.

'Thank you, but I fear that's a bit late for me. I've been travelling much of the day, and I'm feeling rather tired.'

He reached out a hand and touched her elbow, his smile never faltering. 'Well, perhaps another time. I would be delighted to learn more about the beautiful Leda.'

The way he said her name should have made her melt inside, but there was something she couldn't quite put her finger on that didn't seem to ring true. She turned away with an apologetic smile, and hurried back along the corridor. A flirtation with Iannis was just the sort of thing Aunt Ronnie advised. Leda was sure he would have a beguiling line of chat, and it could do her ego the world of good.

But another face was intruding into her consciousness — an open, cheeky visage that had tugged at something she'd thought was dormant. Not as handsome as Iannis, but attractive in a way she found intriguing.

Shaking her head at these unwanted thoughts, Leda hurried down the stairs and back to her cabin. There she felt she could finally allow herself to give into the fatigue that was beginning to engulf her mind and body.

★   ★   ★

Ronnie was still asleep when Leda woke early next morning. She stretched, feeling a little stiff and deciding a run would loosen her up. Pulling on her shorts and a vest top, she looked out her running shoes. Ronnie was just waking as she twisted her long dark hair into a clip, so she explained she would be back in half an hour.

'What about your rendezvous last night?'

Leda sighed. 'No one there. At least, I don't think so. I did see that good-looking Greek officer, Iannis. He offered to take me for a drink when he got off duty at midnight, but I declined as I was beginning to feel tired. I'm sure he wasn't the person I was to meet, as he was definitely surprised when he saw me waiting there.'

'Maybe you should have stayed up a bit later.' Ronnie said with a wicked smile.

'Aunt Ronnie! You are incorrigible!'

Her aunt swung her legs to the floor and reached for her dressing gown. 'No, my dear, you were right. No point exhausting yourself on the first day. There's plenty time to have fun.'

'I don't think I'm ready for romance.'

Ronnie smiled at her affectionately. 'You just enjoy yourself, Leda. That's all I want from you.'

It was still early, and when Leda emerged on to the Promenade Deck, the sun was low on the sea. Marvelling at the steady motion of the ship as it carved through the placid blue waters, Leda took a few deep breaths of invigorating air, so far from land, away from traffic and industry.

There were a couple of other runners ahead of her, and one or two couples taking a brisk early morning walk. Leda set off at a steady jog, appreciating the sparkling of the sun on the rippling water. It was a perfect day. Two or three people were already on loungers soaking up the sun before it became too hot.

As she rounded the stern on her third time round the deck, she felt her heart lurch as she recognised the tall brown-haired man stretched out on a lounger beside the rail. He was writing in a notebook, lost in concentration. Speeding up her pace, she thought she would manage to get by him without him noticing, but he looked up.

'Well, the charming Leda is swanning past.'

Pulling up short, she felt a little frisson of annoyance at his reference to swans. 'I should have known you'd know the origin of my name.'

'Leda, seduced by Zeus in the form of a swan so that she bore him two children. Some versions of the myth say she laid two eggs.'

Her mood of wellbeing thoroughly destroyed, she faced him defensively, her arms folded. 'Well, I'm not being seduced by anyone,' she announced, trying not to blush, 'And I'm certainly not going to be laying any eggs. What are you doing here so early?'

He folded his notebook away, so she couldn't see what he'd written. He had whipped off his glasses the moment he saw her. A touch of vanity, she wondered? 'No, just putting some thoughts down on paper. I like to work early in the day.'

'Ah-ha! So you really are a crime fiction geek.'

Nick's face closed up immediately. 'What do you mean by that?'

Satisfied that at last she had penetrated his easy exterior, Leda leaned one arm on the rail, looking down at him. 'Oh, you know, someone who thinks they're going to write the next bestseller and make pots of money. What *do* you do for a living, anyway?'

He looked away, unwilling to meet

her eyes. 'You could say that I'm a freelance lawyer. I used to work for a big city firm in London, but it wasn't for me. I live out in the sticks now, in Derbyshire.'

'In one of those lovely stone cottages in a little village?' Leda couldn't keep the incredulity from her voice. She had thought he was definitely the City type, not someone who'd opt for the country.

He turned to her, his face open and smiling again. 'Yes, it's true. I have a dog, a black labrador called Maisie, and we can walk into the Peaks straight from the back door. My neighbour's looking after her at the moment.'

Leda looked into his eyes and saw something there that stirred her heart. A sense of peace and contentment radiated from him, which she envied. Catching her breath, not wishing to dissolve her barriers yet, she turned away.

'Time's getting on. Aunt Ronnie will be ready for breakfast. I'd better go.'

Forcing herself not to look back, she

set off at a brisk jog, trying to ignore the pounding of her heart, which hadn't been caused by her exercise.

4

Leda didn't mention her encounter when she returned to the cabin. She needed to work out what it had meant to her first. Once she'd showered and changed, she took her great aunt to the breakfast buffet, and settled her at a table with her choice of food. As Leda sat with her own plate, she asked, 'So, what's in store for today?'

Ronnie cut a little piece of bacon and added some scrambled egg to her fork. 'Well, this is a day at sea as we have to cross the Mediterranean to get to our first port of call on Corsica. But there's plenty to do on the ship — there's a talk about all the different ports we're visiting, at half past ten, after the lifeboat drill. Then there's a choice of writing workshops — either *New Trends in Crime Fiction* or *Forensic Matters*. I think I'll go to the first one.

What about you?'

Leda laughed, shaking her head, then took a sip of orange juice. 'I'll come to the Ports of Call, but after that it's a sun lounger for me, if you don't mind. I want to soak up some of that gorgeous Mediterranean sun.'

★ ★ ★

When they reached the Hollywood Entertainment Lounge, Leda took a sharp intake of breath when she saw the handsome Iannis, greeting people as they took their seats for the talk. His face changed when he saw them. She hoped he wouldn't mention their earlier encounter.

'Dear ladies — the lovely Leda and your aunt. How delightful to see you.'

He shook hands with Ronnie first, then with Leda. His touch lingered a few seconds longer, his dark eyes mesmerising her. Somehow it wasn't creepy like with Jason Rundle. His attention seemed to be gallant, and she couldn't deny that it felt good, even though she was sure it wasn't real. When he dropped her hand, her cheeks grew pink as she wondered if anyone had noticed.

'I am so glad you are thinking of taking some excursions. They are fantastic! Enjoy the talk.'

They thanked him and continued on their way to join the other people in the lounge, but as she passed him, she heard a deep whisper. 'I still long for your company, dear Leda. Come to the New Orleans Jazz Bar at eleven o'clock tonight so that I can learn so much more about you.'

Leda turned her head swiftly to look at him, but he had already directed his gaze to another couple coming in behind them. Taking Aunt Ronnie's arm she steered her into the lounge, where they found two vacant seats near the platform.

'Well,' Ronnie said as they sat down, 'I think I shall have to find some problem for Iannis to solve.' Her eyes twinkled as she looked at Leda.

'Auntie, behave! First you try and fix me up with a writing geek, and now you're making eyes at a good-looking Greek crew member,' she teased. She didn't mention the whispered invitation. She certainly wasn't going to meet him . . . was she?

'Oh, not for me, my dear. Now you have a choice. How exciting!'

They stopped their discussion as the giant screen at the back of the stage came to life, heralding the start of the presentation.

Slides of sun-bleached villages began to appear on the screen, accompanied by Spanish guitar music played through the loudspeakers. One of the excursion officers strolled on stage in her smart ruby uniform, a red and blue scarf tied pertly at her neck. Soon she was asking them all if they were enjoying their first day, and there were enthusiastic calls of 'Yes!' from the crowd. Then she plunged into the talk, explaining some background about each port of call in turn, and the different trips available to book. These varied from active excursions such as biking tours, to sedate trips for the less able, where the passengers would be taken everywhere by bus.

Leda was surprised at how interesting she found the talk, and felt happy anticipation of all the places they would visit — Ajaccio on Corsica, then Rome, the third port near Florence or Pisa, the next call to Villefranche where they could reach either Nice or Monaco, and finally Barcelona.

When the presentation was over, she and Ronnie chatted about what they would like to do, and decided to sign up for the trips to Rome and Florence immediately, knowing the buses would soon book up. They would dock at some distance from the ports, so going by buses organised by the cruise company was by far the easiest option.

Outside the Hollywood Lounge there was a display outlining all the talks and workshops for the Crime cruise. Ronnie browsed for a while, picking up a leaflet. At the top was a photograph of Harry Agnew, the bestselling crime author who was to talk after dinner on the last evening, and whose book her aunt was avidly reading. Leda glanced at the picture of his bearded face and shook her head. That sort of thing wasn't for her. Aunt Ronnie was enthusiastic about the event, but Leda suspected that on the last evening she would prefer to go to one of the bars to have a drink and listen to the music.

Having dispatched Ronnie to her first lecture, Leda changed into her swimsuit with a tunic on top, grabbed a towel and packed a canvas shoulder bag with her MP3 player, mobile phone and a novel she'd picked up at the airport. Sunglasses, a hat, suntan lotion, a bottle of water, and she was all set.

She managed to find a free lounger near the stern of the ship. It wasn't the best location, the top spots having been snapped up early by sun-worshippers, but she was happy enough to sink back with her eyes closed, listening to some of her favourite music, and letting the warmth of the sun penetrate her bones.

Of Nick Drake there was no sign. Maybe he was skulking in his cabin with his fantasies of being a famous author.

She must have dozed off for a while, but then she became aware of low voices speaking urgently close by.

' . . . it's all in place. You know what you have to do.' It was a man's voice.

'But I don't want to. I'm scared. Don't make me . . . ' a woman replied.

Leda blinked, opening her eyes suddenly. Had she really heard that? The woman had sounded really frightened. Blinking in the brightness of the sun, even with her sunglasses on, she turned her head, and could see a couple walking away. Like so many others, the woman had dyed blonde hair. It could be anyone — but somehow it looked rather like Tish Rundle, and the man could be her husband Jason. They rounded a corner and were gone, and

55

she didn't have the chance to find out.

She reached into her bag for her water bottle, took a sip of water, and retrieved her book. Soon she was immersed in the antics of a dizzy young woman careering round Paris, and had obliterated all thoughts of that odd encounter.

★   ★   ★

At lunchtime, Leda forgot to tell Ronnie about the overheard conversation, as her great aunt was eager to tell her all about the crime talk.

As they were leaving the cafeteria, Leda's heart lurched at the sight of Nick walking towards her, his notebook under his arm.

'Leaving already?' He looked disappointed.

'I'm going to have a snooze before my next talk,' Ronnie explained. 'It's the one on Maintaining Suspense. But why don't you stay and have a coffee with Nick, Leda?'

Momentarily thrown by Ronnie's suggestion, Leda couldn't think of any reason why she had to leave, since her Pilates class wasn't until half past three. 'I suppose I could . . . '

Nick's face broke into a delighted grin. 'As long as you don't mind me eating — I'm pretty hungry.'

Leda laughed. 'I can put up with that. Are you all right going to the cabin on your own, Auntie?'

Ronnie assured them she would be fine, and shooed them back into the dining area. Leda served herself a cup of coffee from the machine and joined Nick at the table he'd selected by the window. While he tucked into pasta, she looked through the glass at the waves the ship was ploughing over, rocking the vessel gently.

'I can think of nothing better than eating out on the ocean, watching the sea,' he commented.

'As long as the weather is good — I wouldn't fancy a rough voyage. That was something that deterred me from coming on the cruise, but Ronnie needed me, so I couldn't let her down.'

Nick smiled. 'She's so interested in everything. I hope I'm like that when I'm her age.'

'Yes, it's a pleasure getting to know her better.'

As the minutes went by, Leda was surprised at how easy it was to talk with Nick, after their inauspicious start. The conversation didn't cover anything deep, or even very personal, though they did discuss places they had visited, and found that they had one or two in common.

Nick refilled her coffee and selected a plate of apple pie and custard for himself for dessert.

'How can you eat that on a hot day?' Leda laughed as he eagerly demolished the sweet.

'It's very good,' he announced, clearing the last morsel, which made her smile.

'Will you be at the Captain's Dinner tonight?' she asked him. 'Ronnie is

58

looking forward to it.'

'Not my scene.' He put his empty plate to one side and wiped his mouth with a paper napkin. 'I haven't brought any particularly smart clothes. I'll head back to the cafeteria when I'm hungry.'

She was determined not to let him see the disappointment in her face, so she smiled brightly, and was about to ask him what he was doing for the rest of the day, but at that moment a uniformed officer stepped up to the table.

'Excuse me, sir . . . are you Nicholas Drake?'

Leda looked up. It was Iannis. Her cheeks flushed at both the men who were showing interest in her being in the same place. But she had no time to reflect. A frown creased Nick's forehead as he acknowledged the officer's question.

'Then I must ask you to come to the main information desk, sir. We have an urgent communication for you from England.'

Nick jumped to his feet. 'Of course.' Concern filled his features as he turned to Leda. 'I'm sorry to have to dash off, Leda. We'll have to continue our conversation some other time.'

Feeling bereft, Leda nodded, and watched him thread his way purposefully through the tables in the cafeteria, which were now only sparsely occupied. Then she realised that Iannis was still standing at her side.

'May I sit?' he asked, unexpectedly. At her murmured agreement, he took Nick's empty chair and sat opposite her, his dark eyes gazing into her own. 'I admit I feel rather envious of this Englishman. He seems to have won your heart.'

Leda gave an exclamation. 'Hardly! I've only just met him.' He made it sound as if she was throwing herself at Nick.

Iannis gave a slow smile, showing his perfect teeth. 'That makes me happy. I do not like to feel I have lost you already.'

She began to protest, but he held a finger to her lips, which made her tense. It was a very intimate gesture for someone who was supposed to be in his professional role. Luckily the cafeteria was only sparsely occupied now, so no one was close enough to notice.

'I have a day off tomorrow, and would like to take you to Rome. It is a most wonderful city, one of my favourites. Please let me show it to you.'

Leda felt as if the air had been knocked from her lungs, before she found her voice.

'That's very kind, but my aunt and I are already booked on an excursion.'

He pursed his lips and pulled a sad face. 'I am sorry to hear that. Could not your aunt go on her own? There will be plenty of other people on the tour. Then I could escort you around myself.'

Indignation swirled in her chest. 'No, I can't. Aunt Ronnie is over eighty, I've come on this cruise to accompany her, and we're looking forward to exploring

61

together tomorrow. Now if you'll excuse me, I have a Pilates class.'

She jumped to her feet, but his hand shot out and grasped her arm, preventing her from leaving.

'I have upset you. I apologise sincerely. I meant no insult to your aunt — your great aunt. Indeed, she does not look that old. I hope we may spend some time together another day. I will be in the Jazz Lounge every night from eleven-thirty. My offer of a drink still stands.'

Leda shook her arm free, and allowed her irritation to subside. 'Thank you for your invitation . . . we'll see. I must go now.'

As she walked away, she wondered why she wasn't jumping at the chance to spend time with this charming, handsome officer. There was just something she couldn't quite put her finger on that didn't pull her in.

In contrast, she was beginning to be intrigued by Nick, even though she had found him annoying at first. He didn't have the slick good looks of Iannis, but he was somehow more attractive. There was also an air of mystery about him — he seemed to be hiding something. Her curiosity was piqued.

Leda shook herself and pulled her shoulders back. It was time to release any thoughts of romance, knowing her past record.

She would enjoy her class and the dinner this evening, as she didn't need a man to make her cruise experience a good one.

★   ★   ★

After Leda's Pilates class, Ronnie greeted her in the cabin with the cruise schedule for the day.

'Look, I've just noticed there's a tour backstage in the Hollywood Lounge where they do the big evening shows. Apparently there's no show tonight as they have a visiting stand-up comedian, and the entertainment group have a night off.'

63

'Aren't you tired after your talk, Ronnie?' Leda slipped off her Lycra gear and pulled on her cropped trousers and short-sleeved blouse.

'I confess I didn't go. I fell asleep and missed the beginning and I thought it would be impolite to walk in after it had started. I'm in the mood to do something rather than just sit around until it's time to change for dinner. We still have a couple of hours before the drinks reception.'

Leda released her hair from the ponytail she had pulled it into for the exercise class, and ran a comb through her dark locks.

'No letters or messages today?'

'No, I haven't seen anything. I wonder if your secret admirer will contact you again?'

'To be honest, I'm glad there's been nothing more. It was a strange situation, and I'd rather have a straightforward holiday. It's enough to be on a crime writing themed cruise, without my own personal mystery to deal with.'

The tour started soon, so they headed for the Hollywood Lounge, where a group of eight people had gathered — among them a couple with two young girls, both of whom chattered excitedly about the forthcoming tour.

A young woman with her hair piled on top of her head and wearing white shorts, took their names, writing them on a clipboard. Ronnie walked up to her to tell her who they were. Head bowed, the woman scratched the names on her paper, but then turned away quickly, saying, 'Excuse me!' and hurried beyond the door marked Crew Only.

The passengers introduced themselves to each other while they waited for the young woman to return. Another female passenger arrived, saying that she was relieved not to have missed the deadline. Although they kept glancing towards the door, there was no sign of the woman.

The mother of the two girls looked at

her watch, and turned to Leda 'I make it almost half past four. What about you?'

Leda agreed. 'Have they forgotten about us?'

'Not after taking our names,' an elderly man grumbled. 'If she's much longer, I'm giving up. It's too glorious a day out there to be cooped up waiting for something that isn't going to happen.'

By now Ronnie was sitting in the first row of theatre seats chatting to another white-haired woman. When the door swung open again they all looked up eagerly. This time it was a slim, fit young man with dark hair, who looked like he was one of the dancing troupe.

He smiled at them uncertainly. 'Hi, guys, I'm Ashton. I'm going to take over from Chloe, as I'm afraid she's feeling unwell. Sorry to have kept you waiting.'

'We're so sorry to hear about Chloe — is she the dancer who took our names?' The girls' mother put an arm

66

round each daughter as they moved forward at Ashton's gesture.

'Yeah. She sends her apologies. Don't worry,' he grinned, 'I'll show you all the interesting stuff. Now, how many are we . . . eleven? We can fit you all in backstage. Come through, follow me.'

Leda took Ronnie's arm and joined the group as they filed through the door. Ronnie whispered out of the corner of her mouth, 'Was it something I said? She looked fine until I spoke to her!'

Leda shook her head.

'You obviously frightened the life out of her, Auntie!' she laughed.

For a few moments they both had difficulty paying attention to what Ashton was telling them, but were soon engrossed as he took them through to the wings and regaled them with stories of near-disasters and quick changes, of performing in rough seas and accommodating big celebrities. Then they went through the dressing-rooms and ooh-ed and aah-ed at some of the sparkling costumes and wigs hanging up. He adorned the heads of the little girls with huge feathered headdresses, which caused much giggling from the two.

After that they all went up on stage, and the two youngest members of the group had the chance to perform a dance. They all applauded, including Ashton, and the girls gazed at him with adoring eyes as he told them they should apply to the cruise company when they were older.

'That was nice of him,' Leda commented once the tour was over and were dispersing. 'I don't think we could have had a better guide.'

'No, he was excellent. We must come to one of the shows now we've seen what goes on backstage.'

A small group of musicians was now setting up on the stage, no doubt in connection with the evening's reception.

5

They had almost forty-five minutes to get ready for the Captain's Dinner, the trademark black tie event of the cruise. Just after six o'clock, the two of them were waiting in a long queue of people dressed in their finery. *What a song and dance!* Leda thought.

All this dressing up and having photos taken with the captain was a little over-the-top, but Ronnie was thrilled at the prospect, having put on her best silk two-piece in a delicate lavender. Leda was wore a mid-calf red satin dress with shoestring straps, and stiletto sandals, and had to admit she didn't often get the chance of a glamorous evening out!

First they were photographed together in front of a painted backdrop of a moonlit deck scene, then they were in a line waiting to shake hands with the captain. Leda watched with amusement as a grey-haired couple in evening dress eagerly greeted Captain Romero, a tall Italian with greying hair and patrician features. *How does he keep up being friendly to hundreds of people?* Leda wondered as he laughed at something the man said to him, before another photographer stepped in and took their picture.

Then it was their turn and Captain Romero turned on his Italian charm, flashing white teeth and greeting them affably. Ronnie thanked him for his skills in sailing the Ocean Star, at which he laughed readily.

'I do my best, but the good weather is nothing to do with me, I confess!'

Leda didn't mind when he put an arm around their shoulders for the photograph. He seemed a pleasant man, doing his job — and Ronnie would probably like the photo as a memento.

What a pity Nick wouldn't be at the dinner, Leda mused as she took a pre-dinner cocktail, laid on as part of the evening. He would look good in a smart suit, she thought. No, she mustn't start thinking about him. Anyway, he said it wasn't his sort of thing, so she wouldn't allow him to intrude into her mind any more this evening.

The stage was occupied by the quintet they had seen earlier, playing gentle easy-listening numbers. The music wasn't loud so people filing into the lounge could chat easily.

Once everyone had taken their seats, the Captain came on stage to deliver a welcoming speech, then he introduced them to Iannis, who was standing just behind him, and other crew members. One by one the crew came on stage accompanied by applause from the passengers.

Once this was over, the passengers were given notice to proceed to the dining room. Expecting to sit with the Rundles again for the meal, Leda was surprised when another couple joined them.

'Hello, I'm Steve,' the man said, giving each of them a strong handshake. The smile in his tanned face was ready and relaxed.

'I'm Jackie,' his wife added, also shaking their hands and pulling her chair in as she sat down. She had auburn-tinted hair in a long page-boy style, dark eyes twinkled beneath her fringe, and a laugh was never far from her lips. She wore a turquoise satin dress with plunging neckline that showed off an impressive tanned cleavage.

Leda warmed to their friendly approach at once.

They said they had travelled from Glasgow. Jackie had a pronounced Scottish accent, though Steve said he was originally from Sheffield, and the Yorkshire twang was still perceptible.

'This is the first cruise for both of us,' Ronnie explained as she drained the last of her champagne cocktail. 'I didn't try it before because my late husband wasn't keen on stepping off dry land

— or on dressing up.'

Jackie giggled. 'You'll never guess how many cruises we've been on — twenty!'

At their companions' astonished expressions, Steve laughed. 'This is number twenty-one. We love it! We've cruised the Adriatic, the Aegean, the Caribbean, you name it! This is our fourth time in the Med.'

'You can't beat a cruise for a relaxing holiday, and seeing the world.'

Steve reached out and took his wife's hand, regarding her with a fond expression. 'Yes, it's a great way to get away from our full-on jobs.'

'What do you do?' Leda asked.

The couple eyed each other with a little smile. 'I don't know if we should tell you — we were with a different couple last night, and they didn't seem to like it at all. They even asked to change tables!' Jackie told them with a disbelieving laugh.

'The Rundles?' Leda exclaimed.

'Yes, that's the name . . . strange pair.'

'I can't believe it!' Ronnie added. 'We ended up sitting with them.'

'So what *do* you do?' Leda asked.

'Well, I know appearances can be deceptive, but Jackie here is a top-notch lawyer with a big firm in Glasgow, and I'm a TV researcher, for a programme by an investigative reporter.'

'Wow! That sounds fascinating!' Leda was delighted. 'I'd love to hear more. I wonder why the Rundles didn't?'

'Remember they said they were from a humble background . . . office workers?' Ronnie said.

'Maybe that's it,' Jackie said.

Leda found their chat fascinating. Steve and Jackie didn't say much more about their work, but had interesting stories about their other cruises.

'So why did you come on a crime writing cruise if you wanted to get away from your everyday lives?' Ronnie eventually asked.

Steve's expression was abashed. 'Well, if you really want to know, I've written a couple of crime novels myself, but I haven't managed to find a publisher yet. I'm hoping to pick up some tips.'

'That's marvellous!' Ronnie looked impressed. 'I'm an avid reader, so I'm enjoying the talks — and my current favourite author, Harry Agnew, is the keynote speaker on the final evening.'

Jackie nudged her husband and laughed. 'You've got company, then — Steve likes his style, and hopes to get some inspiration.'

'I'd be glad to get one novel published, never mind nine!' Steve emptied the last of their wine bottle into their two glasses.

By the end of the dinner, they took Ronnie's mobile phone number and agreed to let her know if Steve managed to succeed in his aspirations. Leda was sorry to part company with them, feeling so relaxed in their company.

'I wish we could sit with you every evening.'

Jackie shook her head. 'Unfortunately it's just for the Captain's Dinner night.

We go back to our usual tables for the rest of the week.'

Ronnie hugged them both. 'Well, I hope we'll meet again during the cruise. It's been a pleasure — and I look forward to news about that novel.'

As they left the dining room they noticed the Rundles sitting with two elderly ladies. They looked happy enough, Jason obviously in the middle of a story, waving his arms as he talked.

'Do you fancy going up to the cafeteria for a cup of tea, Auntie?'

Ronnie agreed, as only coffee had been available after the dinner, so they retrieved warmer cardigans from their cabin before taking the lift up to the cafeteria deck.

In the back of Leda's mind when she suggested it was the thought that Nick might be there. After all, he seemed to like eating late, if lunch was anything to go by. But when there was no sign of him, she couldn't help feeling a little flat, despite their enjoyable evening with Jackie and Steve.

As she went to bed later, she was cross with herself for letting this take the shine off the evening. There hadn't even been a glimpse of the smooth Iannis in his delectably smart white uniform.

For a moment she considered taking up his offer to meet for a drink in the Jazz Lounge, but on second thoughts she decided not to. He could well have made the same offer to several unaccompanied women on the cruise, and she didn't want to become one of a harem. She was done with relationships . . . and her life was full enough.

6

When they woke the next morning, they saw land through their porthole as the ship approached Corsica.

Leda went for her usual run while the ship was docking, so she would be early enough to take Aunt Ronnie for breakfast. Although she was thinking about what they would do in Ajaccio, her eyes were scanning the people on deck.

Passengers were already taking photographs as the Ocean Star moved into its berth on the quayside, right in the centre of the town. The shouts of the crew and the clank of machinery accompanied Leda as she made her way round the deck. But she reached the entrance nearest their cabin, and pushed open the heavy door to step back inside, without seeing any sign of the tall figure with the notebook sitting in the early morning brightness. A little cloud of disappointment settled on her, though she tried to banish it.

Breakfast over, Leda and Ronnie stood on deck in the warm sunshine, watching other passengers disembark to the organised coach trips. The two women gazed over the palm tree lined promenade that led to the centre of the town. From here they could see tall blocks of buildings painted in shades of pink and cream, with contrasting shutters and wrought iron balconies. It looked delightfully continental, espe-cially with the white hulls and masts of the yachts moored alongside.

'I think it will be much better for us just to have a gentle day, exploring the town.' Ronnie took a sheet of paper from her handbag. 'Tomorrow and the day after, we're signed up for two long days, so it would be pleasant just to relax today. It says in the information here that there's a tourist bus we can take along the coast to a viewpoint. Then we could wander round the town a little, have lunch on shore or back on the ship.'

There were marquees along the quayside, with banners announcing that the yacht club of the Mediterranean was having its annual meeting there. The tall white yachts anchored at the quay, with groups of people working on deck, were an attractive addition to the scene. It looked idyllic, and Leda felt a lift of excitement at the prospect of visiting the shore.

They only had to walk down a short gangplank to reach the quayside. In the marquees there was a bar, and displays from the sponsors of the event, a luxury car manufacturer. By the time Leda and Ronnie had sauntered along the promenade, they were in the centre of the town, which was right on the seafront. They paused to appreciate a powerful sculpture commemorating the members of the Resistance who had fought in Corsica during the Second World War.

They soon located the tourist bus

that had just come in and was disgorging a group of sightseers. Leda spotted a little booth beside the bus stop, where she asked for two tickets in her best French.

'Do you know, Aunt Ronnie, he immediately replied to me in English,' she complained as she rejoined her aunt with the tickets. 'I didn't think my accent was that bad!'

Ronnie laughed. 'It's plain from your appearance that you're a tourist, dear. In any case, you don't have a Corsican accent.'

Leda smiled, feeling mollified. The bus doors opened and they climbed on board, but Ronnie declined to tackle the stairs to the upper deck, saying it was too much for her arthritic knees. They still had a wonderful view of the coast as the bus trundled along.

The countryside looked so wild, that they could imagine how the Resistance had managed to survive so long during wartime. This was a rugged, beautiful coastline, with traditional villages and new hotels, as well as occasional cemeteries which looked like small villages of houses for the departed. On their other side, the Mediterranean was a warm blue, calm and inviting.

Leda let her thoughts wander as they sat taking in the views. It had been a strange two days. It disturbed her that Nick Drake intruded into her thoughts. At one moment she felt annoyed by his teasing, the next acknowledging that she found him attractive. She found his conversation interesting, and was keen to know more, although he had glossed over his work and home life when she asked. He had declared he was on holiday and wanted to get away from it all. Was she being too suspicious, or was he hiding something?

The bus drew to a halt at an empty car park beside a closed restaurant. From here a rugged spit of land led to a small tower.

There were fifteen people on the bus. The younger ones disembarked immediately, and began the walk out to the tower. The passengers had about twenty minutes before the bus left for the return journey. Ronnie and Leda strolled down to the shore along the paved part of the path, enjoying the warmth of the sun.

Ronnie regarded the closed restaurant with a frown. 'It would have been nice to sit and enjoy a cool drink. There's not even a seat here.'

'It must only open evenings,' Leda concluded.

After a short wander they returned to the bus. The other tourists were still exploring and Leda saw them scrambling over the rough terrain, but wasn't tempted to follow, happy to sit with Ronnie.

Then her mood of content was interrupted when Ronnie's voice intruded into her reverie.

'I think it's time we had a little talk, dear.'

Oh, no! Ronnie was in one of her advice modes. Leda suppressed a groan.

'You know I only have your best

interests at heart. I want you to be happy. You've let that Damian spoil your life. I know he pushed you around and destroyed your self-confidence, but after all this time you must let go of it. You have a big heart, and must let yourself love again.'

'Oh, Auntie. You're mistaken. I just haven't found anyone yet.'

'I remember when I saw you soon after you split up. All the light had gone out of you. But it's been over a year and you're full of life, and you have passion in you. But you've let it all dry up — or else have channelled it into your work.'

Leda said nothing, stunned. She had no idea Aunt Ronnie had been watching her so closely.

'Your mother is my only niece, and I've always had a soft spot for her. And I feel the same for you, Leda. You're like a granddaughter to me, as Bill and I were never blessed with children. You have to make the most of life — don't let it pass you by. It's all very well having a good career, but if you cut

84

yourself off from love, you will have a big hole in your life.'

Leda felt tears prick her eyes. It was true, she had to admit it. Much as she loved her work, her friends and activities, it just wasn't the same without someone special to share it with. She looked into her great aunt's face.

'I know, Auntie. But it's hard. I find it difficult to trust a man now.'

Ronnie took her hand. 'Don't feel it has to be true love straight away. I know you were with Damien for a while, and you thought it would last. But why not just have a fling to let you feel good about yourself? A cruise is the ideal place for that. Plenty of opportunity for socialising, just enjoying being with the opposite sex. Already we've met two attractive men, and there could be more!'

Leda burst out laughing. 'You must have been a real raver before you married Uncle Bill!'

Ronnie chuckled. 'I don't feel at all old inside. It's just the outside that has gone downhill.'

Leda leaned over and gave her a hug. 'All right, Auntie, I'll try to have fun.'

'You could start with that nice young man, Nicholas. I can see he's interested in you.'

Leda blushed. 'He's not made any sort of romantic move. We just chatted yesterday.'

But inside she was thinking if her aunt had noticed his interest, then maybe it was true.

She perceived a little smile on Ronnie's lips, but there was no reply as at that moment a group of people climbed back on board the bus, followed by the rest of the passengers, and the driver.

The journey back was even more beautiful, as the wind had whipped up and the yachts were now tacking back and forth on the blue waters of the Mediterranean.

No more was said about what they discussed at the stop as they weaved through streets of pink and buff-coloured houses, topped with mellow

86

red roofs. They wandered up the main boulevard, looking at the old buildings and the statue of Napoleon in the park before they returned to the ship for lunch.

As they stepped out of the lift to their cabin, they almost bumped into Iannis.

'Good morning, ladies. Enjoying your day?'

Leda felt Ronnie's elbow dig into her ribs, and realised her aunt wanted her to do the talking.

'Yes, we've had a lovely morning,' she managed to stammer. 'We took a bus trip along the coast and stopped at an old tower on a promontory. It was a beautiful run, and the yachts were out sailing when we returned.'

Iannis's white smile became even wider.

'We are lucky the yacht club is in port these few days. And what are you doing now?'

'Back to the cabin before lunch, and then a relaxing afternoon.'

'Well, it has been lovely to see you

both again. Remember, you can join me in the Jazz Bar after half past eleven to relax with a drink at the end of a busy day. Enjoy the rest of your day.'

With a flash of white teeth, dark eyes crinkling in pleasure, he waved them towards their cabin, and walked away on long, athletic legs.

Ronnie gave Leda a wink. 'See what I mean? He's smitten too! He's even given you an invitation to join him — after dark.'

'Oh, Auntie! You're incorrigible. He's only making passengers feel happy. Let's dump our bags and go for lunch. And no more matchmaking!'

Despite her stern words she laughed, and as she slotted the card into the cabin door, she realised she was actually enjoying herself.

★   ★   ★

While they were eating at the outdoor grill, a shrill voice cut in on their conversation.

'Hello! Have you had a good morning?'

Leda looked up, shading her eyes, to see Tish Rundle, wearing a bright pink see-through wrap that barely covered a bikini of the same colour. From her skin, it was clear she'd been spent all morning in the sun. Her cheeks and nose were an alarming shade of red, which didn't go well with the bright pink ensemble.

Ronnie, charming as always, smiled. 'We did indeed, my dear. We took a trip along the coast in the bus from town. The views were delightful.'

At that moment, Jason Rundle joined them. Being darker in colouring, he was beginning to show a pleasant glow of tan, unlike his wife.

'How nice to see you ladies. We've just been chilling out on deck. We managed to bag two sun-loungers in a great position. We're taking back some food, before anyone else pinches them!' He gave a loud, hearty laugh, which caused people around them to turn their heads. Leda's toes curled in embarrassment.

At that moment, Tish's eyes narrowed.

'Who's that gorgeous man at the bar? Didn't I see you talking to him yesterday?'

Already feeling a guilty flush creeping into her cheeks, Leda saw Tish was staring straight at Nick Drake, who was drinking a long glass of fruit cocktail. He was facing the opposite way, and she hoped he wouldn't notice them and come over.

Jason took Tish's arm and steered her away. 'Come on, darling, stop feasting your eyes.'

Nick looked lost in thought and never turned in their direction. As Leda looked up, he was gone.

★   ★   ★

That afternoon, they relaxed on deck, Ronnie snoozing in the shade while Leda topped up her tan. She was listening to music when a woman's voice penetrated her consciousness.

'Hello, you sun-worshippers! Are you coming for afternoon tea?'

Leda's eyes flew open, recognising the Scottish accent. Jackie and Steve stood beside them.

'That sounds like a marvellous idea,' Ronnie replied, replacing her Harry Agnew murder mystery novel in her bag.

'After that lunch? How can you manage?' Leda pushed her sunglasses up on her head and sat up on her sunbed.

Jackie and Steve laughed. She was wearing a long sarong-style skirt with large blue and yellow flowers and a blue sleeveless blouse. Steve was in a Hawaiian shirt in turquoise and orange, with black shorts. They looked sun-kissed and happy.

'We have to make the most of all the facilities,' Steve replied. 'The afternoon teas on these cruises are not to be missed — a real treat.'

Ronnie swung her legs on to the deck, and declared she had to get the very best out of the cruise, so she would join them.

Leda laughed. 'I think I'll have a swim instead, if I can avoid the eagle eyes of a certain person.' This time she wanted to enjoy herself without any comments from Nick — at least, that's what she told herself.

Ronnie shook her head, and went with Jackie and Steve to the Ocean Spray Lounge where tiny sandwiches and bite-sized cakes were on offer.

* * *

After her swim, Leda returned to their cabin to change. Ronnie was still out, so she put on a clean sun dress and went off in search of her.

It didn't take long to locate her great aunt. She was in the lounge, with a cup of tea in her hand, engrossed in conversation — with Nick Drake!

Leda felt her breath catch in her

throat at the sight of his thick, tousled hair and his smile with strong, even teeth. She turned on her heel, and walked to the window, looking out at the blue sea as it foamed past. Her heart was beating faster. No, she would not let him disturb her. Putting her best smile on her face, she walked into the lounge, trying to look as relaxed as possible.

'I see you've found an admirer, Aunt Ronnie.'

Ronnie looked up, her face full of mischief.

'Jackie and Steve went off to play deck tennis. Steve wants to attend a talk before dinner — I forget what — but he thought it would be useful for his novel. I spotted this nice young man all on his own, so I thought he might like some company.'

Nick jumped to his feet at Leda's appearance, and immediately found another chair to pull up to the little table.

'Your aunt was keeping me right on

the history of crime novels. She's read a lot. I'm very impressed.'

'I've had a lot of years to indulge in my reading, and thankfully my husband was a reader, too, so we used to discuss the books we liked.'

At that moment the waiter came up with a fresh cup and a pot of tea. 'Tea, madam?' he asked Leda in that polite manner that was characteristic of all the staff on the ship.

Leda declined politely. 'Though I might be tempted by one of those tiny cakes. That looks delicious.' She indicated the dainty morsel sitting on Nick's plate, a delicate little sponge sandwich with a sliver of strawberry on the top.

'I'll get you one. They have blackberry, strawberry or mandarin. Which would you prefer?'

Feeling quite pampered, she replied, 'Why don't I try them all? They're small enough!'

He grinned. 'It's good to know you're not one of these girls who spends all her time counting calories. Cakes coming up, pronto!'

Ronnie gave her a twinkling look as Nick disappeared to the buffet. 'I'm glad you're heeding my advice. He's a nice man, and I think you need some attention.'

Feeling self-conscious, Leda shrugged. 'I don't know quite how to take him, but I'm going to try and be more forgiving.' She didn't mention the flutter of excitement in her whenever he was near.

The three of them spent a pleasant hour chatting in the comfortable lounge. Then Ronnie said she had to look out clothes for that evening.

'I'll come with you.' Leda jumped to her feet, suddenly afraid of being alone with Nick, though she couldn't quite judge why.

'No, I'll have a little quiet time. It only takes you a moment to throw on something nice, and look wonderful. It takes a bit longer at my age.'

Alone together, despite the chatter of people around them, a silence fell between Leda and Nick, each conscious of the other's presence. After Ronnie's talk earlier, Leda had begun to acknowledge that she found him extremely attractive, and wasn't sure how to react. Then she recalled how he had rushed off yesterday with an urgent message.

'I hope you didn't get bad news yesterday. You looked concerned when you left the cafeteria.'

Nick blinked a few times, and there was a slight pause as if he was considering how to answer. 'No, it was just work. I managed to sort it out.'

'I thought you were on holiday — it must be annoying to be contacted when you're trying to get away from it all.'

This made him laugh, although she had no idea why. 'No, not this time — I had some stuff that needed sorting, but I can relax now.' Then he abruptly changed the subject. 'Your aunt told me about your business. It sounds as if you're making a good start.'

He obviously didn't want to talk about his work, and he'd told her he was trying to get away from it all, so maybe he was dealing with a stressful law case back home.

Going along with him, Leda answered brightly, 'Yes, I have several commissions lined up. A lot of people now aren't moving house, opting to put their savings into improving their current homes. I have contacts with a builder who does a lot of extension work, and I've had three jobs with him.'

As their conversation led them down different paths, she realised how easy it was to talk to Nick. His teasing manner was in fact very gentle, not threatening as it had been with Damien. It was with some surprise that she realised it was fast approaching six o'clock.

'I'd better go and check on Aunt Ronnie — and I need to change.'

'Are you dining in the formal dining room?'

Leda stood up, picking up her

cardigan. 'Yes, Auntie likes the glamorous trappings. We've been teamed up with a rather odd couple, though.'

'How are they odd?'

She shook her head as they walked to the door of the lounge. 'It's difficult to say. I suppose they're just real characters. They say they adore cruising, though, and I've seen them joining in at a lot of the events. The food is really good in the restaurant. You should try it.'

His face closed a little. 'I don't like formal dining. There's a good choice of meals in the cafeteria right up to midnight, so I can wear my casual clothes and chill out on my own.'

Leda thought it sounded a little sad, when there were so many interesting people to talk to, but she didn't say anything. There was a lot about Nick she didn't know, but perhaps he would elaborate later.

'Well, it's been a nice afternoon. Our cabin's on deck six, so I'll just nip down these stairs.'

His arm shot out and his hand gripped her arm, holding her back. 'Leda . . . would you like to meet for a drink, later? The New Orleans Jazz Bar has some good music in the evening — if that's your type of thing?'

Her breath felt tight in her chest as she looked into his face. This wasn't the casual encounter of their other meetings — this was a real invitation, maybe even a date!

She found her voice. 'Yes . . . I would like that. What time?'

'Ten o'clock — if that's not too late?'

'No, it's perfect.' It was too early for Iannis to be there, so she would be able to relax with Nick. 'Aunt Ronnie will be getting ready for bed, so I can leave her and come up.' Her lips curved, a bubble of excitement forming. 'See you later.'

7

Leda decided not to tell Ronnie immediately about her rendezvous with Nick, revelling in delicious secret anticipation. She would mention it later and slip out when her aunt was preparing for bed. Hugging it to herself, she was determined to enjoy every moment of the evening ahead and be her most sparkling self over dinner.

Tish was still looking pink, her face now shiny with after-sun cream, and her mood bubbly. Jason was in a buoyant mood, too. They described at length the lunchtime entertainment they'd watched, a demonstration of cocktail making with some deft juggling from the bartenders on deck.

'Tell us more about what you do back in England,' Ronnie ventured as they began dessert.

'I have my own business,' Jason replied.

'That's interesting — so do I,' Leda said. 'I'm an interior designer. What do you do?'

'Oh, a bit of this, a bit of that.' His eyes were hooded as he dug his spoon into his meringue. A piece broke off sharply and shot across the table towards Tish, who giggled. There was a short silence, as Jason was clearly not forthcoming about his work.

'Well, I can see you're successful,' Ronnie said to fill the silence. 'What do you do, Tish?'

'She helps me — as a receptionist and assistant.' Jason's tone was curt.

'How nice, to work together.' Leda tried to think of something else, but Jason's shuttered expression made other questions fly from her mind.

Ronnie gallantly changed the subject. 'Are you planning on going to any of the book talks? There's one this evening on building character.'

Tish burst out laughing. 'No, we're

not interested in all this writing business. We just came for the cruise. We're going to the show in the big lounge, then we'll probably go to the karaoke evening in the Captain's bar.'

Conversation moved on to their favourite songs, so the awkward moment passed.

'I like the sound of the show,' Ronnie said as they laid their serviettes on the table and stood to leave. 'It's in the Hollywood Lounge, isn't it?'

Tish swung round and gave her a scowl.

'I don't think it's your sort of thing. It'll be too loud and bright for an older person.'

Stung by this insult to her aunt, Leda sprang to her defence.

'What nonsense! The entertainments are for everyone. And Ronnie has a very young outlook!'

Ronnie put her hand on Leda's arm to halt her, and added in a calm voice, 'I think it's for me to decide what I wish to see. I've always loved musical shows with songs and dancing. I believe it will be very entertaining.'

Jason laughed nervously. 'Of course, Tish wasn't being derogatory. I'm sure you'll love it.'

Tish gave a shrill laugh. 'Of course. No offence meant.'

Jason took his wife's hand. 'Come, darling. You're a bit tired after all that sun.' He led her from the dining room, murmuring something in her ear as they went.

Ronnie looked at Leda and raised her eyebrows.

'Let's hurry to the Hollywood Lounge. I want to get a good seat.'

As Leda and Ronnie sat with a glass of wine each, waiting for the show to start, Leda commented, 'They really are a strange couple. Why on earth would she deter you from the show? There are people of all ages in the audience. And that was an odd moment when we asked Jason about his business. He looked really furtive.'

Ronnie looked amused.

'Maybe it's not entirely 'legit', as they say.'

'Do you think so?' Leda was incredulous.

'My dear, sometimes I think you're too innocent. You never seem to see through dodgy people — and you suspect the wrong ones, like poor Nick.'

Leda folded her arms, indignant. 'I don't know what you mean. I just don't always look for bad things. I sometimes think you're too immersed in your crime novels. Maybe Jason wants to leave thoughts of work at home while on holiday.'

At that moment the lights dimmed and music started to pour from the loudspeakers. Ronnie patted her hand, and sat back.

Leda sighed, aware of the tension in her whole body. Maybe Ronnie was right. At least she hadn't taken offence at Leda's comments. Following her aunt's actions, she turned her eyes to the stage as the first of the entertainers walked on stage.

The show was a medley of songs from top West End musicals, and Leda began to relax, her attention captured by the music, dancing and costumes. The girls carried huge feather fans. She felt her creativity beginning to hum, knowing that she had commissions coming up. This could be a great theme for one of the couples who wanted an opulent feel to their new extended bedroom and en-suite. Her hands itched for a pencil and pad. She would scribble down some ideas as soon as they were back in the cabin.

As the lights came up, Ronnie took off her glasses and polished them. 'Well, that was a spectacle. Weren't the dancers good?'

'I was very impressed. I wasn't sure if I could see the young woman who was taken ill before the tour yesterday.'

'My eyesight's not so sharp these days, so they all looked the same to me. I expect she's fine now. I must say, I'd like to come to some of the other scheduled performances.' Ronnie stood up, picking up her bag and stick. 'Well, it's a cup of tea for me, and then bed.'

They went to the cafeteria and it was there that Leda broke the news about her rendezvous with Nick. The delight on Ronnie's face was instantaneous.

'That's wonderful news. What will you wear? You want to look your best.'

Leda shook her head, laughing. 'Auntie, it's just casual. I'll go like this.' She was wearing a pretty summer shift dress with a yellow floral pattern, which set off her dark hair. 'You don't fall in love on a ship-board romance. How can you? We only see each other briefly, and there's no sense of the other person's real life or circumstances. They could be spinning all sorts of stories, and you would have no idea what was the truth.'

Ronnie shook her finger at her. 'There you go again — being negative, analysing.'

'But it's true. This is just a bit of fun. There's no substance to holiday romances — if that's what he has in mind.'

Ronnie gave a snort of disdain. 'Well, if that's all he wants, he should have his head examined. A lovely, attractive, single girl like you — intelligent too. What more could he want?'

In the end, Leda gave in. Ronnie was determined to matchmake, and she was equally determined not to be caught out or led on. She and her aunt would just have to differ.

★ ★ ★

Leda was careful not to be in the bar on the dot of ten o'clock. It would be embarrassing if he was late, and she didn't want to sit on her own. She had let down her hair and brushed it to a glossy ebony sheen, and touched up her lipstick. Subtle, that was what she wanted.

Pausing at the door of the Jazz Lounge, she listened to the music that floated out of the door, relaxed and sultry. It taunted her, drew her in, though she resisted for a moment so she could make sure Nick was there.

Thankfully she recognised his rangy figure sitting at the bar, and saw that he already had a small glass in his hand. She waited until he turned his head away, then slipped through the tables to appear at his side.

'The music is good,' she said softly in his ear over the instrumentalists.

His head whipped round, a smile tugging at his lips. 'You came.' His gaze was soft, which made her feel welcomed. It was a pleasant sensation.

She perched on the stool next to him, swinging her legs round and crossing them gracefully. 'Did you doubt me?' She was in the mood to flirt, something she hadn't done for a very long time.

The corners of his eyes crinkled. 'You're an elusive woman, Leda. I'm not sure you trust me.'

She laughed. 'Well, we're in plenty of company, so if I don't trust you, I can call for help.'

He shook his head. 'Am I really that

fearsome? Come on, what will you have to drink?'

Having ordered her a glass of white wine, they took their drinks to a table in a corner, far enough from the musicians so they could talk. After a while, a few couples got up to dance, and Nick took her hand, pulling her to the tiny dance floor.

'But I don't know how to,' she protested.

'Just follow me.'

He took her arms in a relaxed hold, and steered her round the floor to the slow number. After a few moments Leda began to relax, surprised at his unexpected fluidity on the dance floor. It felt good, being held like this. It had been too long since a man had embraced her, and she began to feel confident in her own attractiveness. His hand came up to stroke her hair on her back, the sensation making her shiver slightly with pleasure. She sighed, her head leaning in so that her cheek touched his chin.

They had another drink, and when the band began to play a more upbeat number, he pulled her up to dance again.

'Well, you're a surprise, Nick Drake! I never expected you to be a dancer.'

'Call that dancing? I just hauled you round the floor a few times.'

She punched his arm gently at his modesty. 'How late does the band stay?'

He looked at his wristwatch. 'Until one, I believe. It's almost midnight now.'

A look of shock passed over her features. 'I'd better go! Aunt Ronnie and I are booked on a trip to Rome tomorrow. It's not a guided tour — they involve a lot of walking — we're to be dropped in the centre, so we can go at our own pace.'

She reached for her bag, and at that moment caught sight of a tall man in the white uniform of a ship's officer sitting at the end of the bar, watching her. Recognising Iannis, her cheeks flamed, and she turned away to hurry after Nick, who was making his way towards the exit.

'I'll walk you back to your cabin,' Nick said.

Once in the corridor, Leda glanced out of the door that led to the deck.

'Look, the moon is almost full, reflecting on the water. Let's go and have a look.'

Without waiting for his reply, she opened the door and stepped over the threshold to head outside. She gave a little shiver in the breeze, surprised when Nick's arm came round her.

'You'll get cold.'

The warmth of his body next to hers brought a blissful sensation of being protected. Softly she murmured, 'We won't be long. Isn't it beautiful?'

They stood by the rail, admiring the view, listening to the sound of the ship cutting through the water. She looked up at him and felt a stab of something she had not felt for a long time as their eyes met. He stroked back a strand of her dark hair that the breeze had whipped across her face. He took a breath, his face coming closer, and she tensed, waiting for their lips to meet . . .

But he turned away. An overwhelming sense of disappointment flooded her. Had he been going to kiss her, or was it her imagination?

They walked back to her cabin, saying nothing. At last she stopped outside the door.

'Have a nice day in Rome tomorrow,' Nick said, touching her cheek briefly.

'Thanks,' she replied, her spirits sinking, still regretting the missed kiss. She swiped her keycard and opened the door a crack. The light was off. 'Goodnight,' she whispered, her voice trembling with disappointment.

He didn't seem to notice. 'Goodnight.' He smiled, and walked off down the corridor. For a moment she watched him, then slipped into the cabin, shutting the door softly behind her.

★   ★   ★

It was difficult getting up in time for her normal morning run, but Leda forced herself out of bed at her usual time and into her shorts and vest. She was glad she had, for the morning was golden and balmy, and it blew away all of her low mood.

It was silly to expect more, she chided herself in time to the pounding of her feet on the deck. It was just a drink in the bar and a couple of dances. Just friendly, nothing more. She wouldn't fall into that trap again.

By the time she returned to the cabin for a shower, she was able to be casual about describing the evening to Aunt Ronnie.

8

The ship docked at Civitavecchia while they were having breakfast. From here they would be taken by bus to Rome. Leda surveyed the information at the main desk as they passed on the way back to their cabin. 'It's going to be hot today. We'd better be prepared.'

They both put on lightweight dresses, taking wide-brimmed hats, sunglasses and sun cream. They also bought a bottle of water each before they disembarked the ship.

Quickly finding their bus, they were soon on the road, with a young female Italian guide informing them of what they could see in the Eternal City. Ronnie had set her heart on visiting the Sistine Chapel, so they knew their first priority was to make their way there.

By the time they reached the centre

of Rome, it was late morning and the sun was beating down relentlessly. Ronnie fanned herself with the information sheet. 'This is probably only pleasantly warm for them — we're just not used to these temperatures.'

The bus stopped right opposite the Vatican. The guide told the passengers their rendezvous point for the return journey was a travel agent's premises facing Saint Peter's Square. While they queued to disembark from the bus, Leda saw the square was full of people.

'Look, Auntie, it's the Pope! He's conducting a service in the open air in the Square!'

They looked on in amazement at the hordes of people thronging the square, all in rapt attention listening to the Pope as he addressed them. Huge images of the aged Pontiff were beamed on to screens around the square so everyone, no matter how far back in the crowd, could see him. The man himself was sheltering under a canopy on the steps of Saint Peter's, with cardinals seated behind him.

The guide explained that the Pope gave a service in the square once a week, and they were lucky enough to have arrived on that very day. The service finished just as they crossed to the square, so they immediately joined a queue for security to search their bags before they entered the Vatican. To get to the Sistine Chapel they would need to buy tickets for the Vatican Museum.

Due to the crowds of visitors, it took them a long time to be vetted and then get to the queue for the museum. It stretched right round the walls of the Vatican. At times there was no shade at all, so they were standing in the full midday sun.

'Are you all right, Auntie?'

Ronnie adjusted her hat for maximum shade. 'I'm sure it won't take much longer to reach the museum. I'm not giving up now that I'm so close to seeing the Sistine Chapel.'

Finally they were inside, where the temperature was considerably cooler. Although there was so much to see in the museum, they had no time to linger, and headed straight for the chapel, as their time in the city was limited. However, they had to follow the prescribed route up and down various staircases, as there was no short cut. It meant they were able to glimpse many treasures, tapestries, and wonderful rooms on the way.

At last they reached their goal. Ronnie managed to find a seat at the side of the chapel, where she could marvel at Michelangelo's depiction of Creation on the famous decorated ceiling. Leda wandered through the crowd, studying every part of the chapel, determined to remember it always.

Then her heart skipped. Surely that was Nick, beside the exit! Who was that man in a suit he was talking to? She turned to check on her aunt. Seeing that Ronnie was still contemplating the ceiling, she turned back, intending to go and say hello. But there was no sign of Nick, or the man in the suit. Had she imagined it?

Leda threaded her way through the people filling the chapel, back to where Ronnie was sitting. At every moment more tourists entered.

'Are you ready to move on now?'

Ronnie tore her eyes away from the magnificent painting. 'Yes, we ought to give other people room. In any case, we should think about finding a city bus tour, so we can fit it in this afternoon.'

There were still a lot of stairs to climb and descend, and rooms to pass through, but finally they made it back to the entrance.

Leda, her arm linked with Ronnie's, kept looking for Nick, still convinced she'd seen him in the chapel, though she said nothing to her aunt. Ronnie would think she was being fanciful. After all, he'd said nothing about visiting the city when they were together last night.

'We're not going to have time to sit down for lunch, as well as the bus tour,' Leda said as they made their way back to Saint Peter's Square. 'What would you prefer to do?'

'Why don't we buy something at one of these booths?' Ronnie pointed to mobile units selling food. They found quite a choice, and both bought a slice of hot pizza and a drink.

As they rounded the corner of the wall, passing the latest people queuing for the museums, they were surprised and delighted to see several couples in wedding outfits walking towards the square. 'They must be going to be blessed by the Pope,' Ronnie commented. 'What a memorable start to their marriage!'

Leda eyed the women's white bridal gowns with an artist's eye, assessing the folds and cut of each one. The couples were mostly holding hands, looking at each other dreamily. Clearly they were inside bubbles of happiness created by their special day.

'Yes, I suppose it must be, if you're religious.'

Mischief crept into Ronnie's voice.

'Will you get married in church?'

Leda swung her head round defensively.

'Who says I'll get married?'

'No one — just asking, dear. Don't those young women look beautiful? I suppose you would go for a proper wedding dress, at least.'

'I've never really thought about it,' Leda replied in a tight voice that gave away the fact that she had done, and often.

Ronnie regarded her shrewdly. 'Now, Leda, you can't tell me an artistic person like you hasn't plenty of ideas about her wedding dress. Even though you haven't found the right person, I believe you're romantic enough to still want to.'

Leda was astonished at this comment and shook her head.

'Auntie, I really don't want to talk about this.'

120

A tight knot of defence formed in her chest. Planning ahead for romance was never a good idea, she was certain. However, she couldn't prevent her gaze following the young couples as they walked towards the Vatican. Just before she and Ronnie crossed the road, one of the brides turned her head and her eyes locked with Leda's. The happiness and contentment in the young woman's expression struck a chord inside her. It was as if she was conveying a message to a woman of her own generation, beamed through her gaze, sharing the supreme happiness she was experiencing on her special day. Ronnie was unaware of the few seconds of connection between the two women from different countries, before the bride turned away, back to the most important person in her life.

Leda forced herself to blink away unexpected tears that threatened to flood her eyes, although she couldn't have explained to anyone why the

Italian bride's glance had stirred such emotion.

Taking Aunt Ronnie's arm felt comforting, and together they faced the traffic careering past. The growl of the cars and buses enveloped Leda as she concentrated on finding a safe moment for them to cross — but the encounter with the bridal couples stayed in her mind long after their brief silent communication.

* * *

Ronnie and Leda passed the travel agent's where they were due to meet their guide again later, and continued to the bus stop where the hop on, hop off tour bus would halt.

Looking at the itinerary in the leaflet, Leda shook her head. 'We're not going to have time to get off and on the bus, as we have to be back here for three-thirty to meet the guide for our trip back to the ship. Shall we just buy a cheaper ticket for staying on the bus for the whole journey?'

Her great aunt agreed. They ate their pizza as they waited, and had only just finished them when the bus drew in. Quickly they wiped their hands on paper serviettes and deposited their rubbish in the bin beside the bus stop.

'This is a marvellous way to see the most famous sights in a short time,' Ronnie commented as they adjusted their headphones and sat back to listen to the commentary.

They breezed past all the significant sights of Rome, including the Colosseum, the Roman Forum, spectacular fountains and various important buildings. Their one disappointment was that they couldn't see the famous Trevi Fountain from the bus. It would have meant disembarking and walking away from the main road down a narrower street, and they needed to make sure they were back in plenty of time for the tour bus back to the ship.

Leda consoled herself by making up her mind to return to Rome another time. There was a legend that throwing a coin in the Trevi fountain meant you would be sure to come back. She wouldn't even have the chance to do that.

They arrived back at the stop near St Peter's Square in good time, and wended their way through the crowds back to the travel agent's. It was also a large souvenir shop, and crowded with tourists.

'Do you think there would be time to go across to see inside Saint Peter's?' Leda wondered.

Ronnie looked across to the square with a doubtful expression. There were still long queues at security.

'Much as I would love to see Michelangelo's famous *Pieta* sculpture in the flesh, so to speak, I couldn't face standing in those queues. My knees are starting to hurt, and it might take too long, as well.'

'If you're happy to wait here, I could run across for a quick peek.'

At Ronnie's agreement, Leda chose

her queue carefully. Luckily it didn't take long to clear the checkpoint. It was hot, running and dodging through the throngs, but she finally reached the steps. She walked briskly round the cathedral, snapping the most important items so she could show her aunt. She gave herself more time to stand and appreciate the famous sculpture by Michelangelo known as the *Pieta*, portraying Christ and his mother after the Crucifixion. Even through its thick bullet-proof glass, the grace of the lines of the milky marble was breathtaking. After taking several photos, she stepped back, glad she had made the effort. But a glance at her watch told her she would have to hurry to be back at the meeting-point for the rendezvous.

Leda became aware of a familiar tall figure a few steps below her. This time it definitely was Nick! She was about to hurry down to tap him on the arm, when she realised he was speaking on his mobile. His voice drifted up to her . . . 'Yes, it's all in place . . . ' There was a pause as he listened to the other person. 'Thankfully, no one has recognised me, and as long as no one realises who I really am, I'll be fine.'

It was like a punch to her chest. Leda backed up the steps quickly before he saw her.

Why was Nick hiding his true identity? Her heart pounding, she descended at the other side of the steps and ran back across the square. Her time in Rome was nearly up, but those few seconds had flooded her mind with doubts about the man who had begun to capture her heart.

The travel agent's and souvenir shop was thronging with people, but she managed to locate Ronnie, who was talking to a middle-aged couple whose bag straps bore yellow stickers with the number 2, as theirs did.

'Leda, this is Ken and Valerie, who are also on our bus.'

Valerie, an attractive woman with dark hair, immediately smiled. 'Isn't it marvellous here? There's so much to

126

see — and so little time.'

Leda nodded, still a little breathless from her dash across the square. Somehow she managed to answer, 'I know. We'll have to come back another time.'

'I sincerely hope so.' Ken had a pleasant, deep voice. 'We should book a weekend break here, so we have time to explore at our leisure.'

At that moment, their guide appeared, waving a yellow paddle with the number 2 on it.

'I think that's our call to assemble.' Ronnie unfolded her stick and led the way. 'Was it worth the rush, seeing Saint Peter's?' she asked Leda as they walked round to re-board their bus.

'Definitely. But, like Ken said, I wish I'd had longer. Still, I took some photos for you. I'll show you on the bus.'

Leda kept her voice light. She didn't want to tell Ronnie about hearing Nick talking on the phone about hiding his true identity.

Ronnie was pleased to see the photos

on the camera, but eventually nodded off as they motored back to the ship. It had been a long day for her. Leda couldn't relax, her mind tussling with reasons why a seemingly open and honest man might want to conceal who he was. Had she misjudged him completely? These thoughts were still gnawing at her when they arrived back, just in time to change for dinner.

★   ★   ★

Ronnie struggled to fasten her gold sandals.

'Oh, dear, look at my ankles. They're really swollen with the heat.'

'Auntie, that's awful. Do they hurt?'

Ronnie sat on the bed, stretching out her legs and rocking her feet back and forth.

'No, but my knees ache. I'm not too good walking in the heat these days.'

Leda wondered if Ronnie should visit the ship's doctor, but her aunt dismissed her fears.

'I'm sure they'll be much better after a good night's sleep. In any case, I'd like to go to the show again tonight. They're doing a nostalgia feature with hits from the forties. If it's anything like last night, it will be a real spectacle.'

At dinner, the Rundles were in fine fettle. They had also been on one of Rome's tour buses.

'The hop-on, hop-off buses are really good,' gushed Tish. 'We bought tickets as soon as we arrived, and did that all day.'

Jason proceeded to give them a blow-by-blow history and description of the Colosseum, which took them through most of the main course. If Leda hadn't been eating, she would have been yawning! Ronnie bravely managed to look interested throughout. Finally, she managed to change the subject.

'Are you planning to go to Florence or Pisa tomorrow?' Ronnie smiled at the waiter as he put down her dessert plate in front of her.

The couple passed a look between them.

'We're not sure,' Tish finally said.

'It's too late to book a tour, now,' Ronnie said.

Jason set his jaw. 'We can make our own way there, but we might just have a relaxing day, sunbathing. Tish likes to top up her tan.'

Tish simpered. The bright redness of two days ago had indeed mellowed, but Leda still thought she ought to go carefully. Still, there was always plenty to do on the ship. 'You could go to one of the workshops or lectures. What's on the programme tomorrow, Aunt Ronnie?'

Ronnie paused in the act of lifting a strawberry to her mouth. 'There's a talk from a publisher in the morning, and in the afternoon there's a workshop on creating the perfect sleuth.'

Jason gave a derisive snort. 'No way! All this crime stuff is a bit ridiculous. In any case, how many of the people who attend these things will ever be published?'

Leda suddenly felt quite defensive, despite her earlier opinion. 'Many are just interested in the genre. They like reading, like Aunt Ronnie. It helps them appreciate the books more.'

'And we get to meet famous authors.' Ronnie laid down her spoon, having polished off the last of her strawberry shortcake. 'I'm really looking forward to seeing Harry Agnew give his talk at the end of the holiday. He's one of my favourites and I hope he'll sign my copy of his latest book.'

Jason looked sceptical, digging his spoon into his fruit tart. Tish shot him a look that Leda could not fathom. Was she agreeing with him silently, or disagreeing? They really were a strange couple!

9

The evening's show was indeed as slick and professional as the previous night. Ronnie clearly enjoyed it, but was looking tired by the end. 'I just want a cup of tea, then I'll turn in.'

Leda felt rather flat as they returned to their cabin. What could she do? It was only ten, and she wasn't ready to sleep yet. Maybe she would go to one of the bars and listen to the music, though she didn't like sitting on her own.

As she opened their cabin door, she spied a note on the floor, which must have been pushed underneath. Was this another message from her mysterious anonymous admirer? Her name was written on the folded sheet of paper . . .

Join me for a bit of moon-gazing on the Promenade Deck at ten o'clock. Nick.

Ronnie was agog to hear what was in the note.

'You must go — wear something a bit dressier. How about that lovely long pale blue dress?'

Leda's heart was beating faster. 'Auntie, it's just a little flirtation.' Besides, she wasn't sure if she could trust him, now she knew he was deliberately hiding something from her.

'Dressing up and flirtation is good for you. After all, this is a holiday, and I want you to have fun — not to be stuck looking after an old lady.'

Flinging her arms round her aunt, Leda exclaimed, 'I don't think of you as an old lady.'

Ronnie gave a little laugh. 'Much as I would love to be able to do all the things you do, I know my limitations. And it's bed for me, now. But it's fun for you. Put on that dress and do your hair.'

In the end, Leda chose a short chiffon dress in white with a gold belt, and left her hair loose. She wore gold gladiator-style sandals, and carried a gold clutch bag.

Ronnie kissed her cheek. 'Off you go and have a good time. I'll hear all about it in the morning.'

Leda felt anticipation coursing through her, and was cross with herself. Yes, she wanted to spend time with Nick, and found him attractive, but she knew so little about him. Why did he want to hide his true identity? Did she have the nerve to ask him about it? She knew this was just a shipboard flirtation, and she had to remain nonchalant. But it had been so long since she had let her heart be penetrated, that she just couldn't subdue the flicker of excitement that had ignited.

As she walked up the stairs, people were coming out of the second performance of the evening's show in the Hollywood Lounge, so she decided to find a quieter route. There was another stairwell further along the deck, beside the casino. On the deck above she had to cut back through the cabin accommodation to reach the exit out on to the Promenade deck.

She glanced at her watch. It was already ten o'clock. Good. She didn't want to be early.

At that very moment, a cabin door opened on her right, and a heavy blow hit her between the shoulder-blades!

Stumbling forward, she couldn't keep her balance, and sprawled onto the carpet, her bag flying off into a corner. Winded, she tried to catch her breath and was vaguely aware of footsteps receding around the corner.

'Leda! Are you all right?'

She barely registered that the voice was familiar, just tried to gather her shaking limbs to sit up. Then she looked up and saw the concerned face of Tish Rundle looking down into hers as she pressed the clutch bag back into her hand.

Leda pushed herself into a sitting position and took a deep breath.

'I think I'm OK . . . what happened?'

Jason appeared. 'A man was hurrying past and knocked you over. Are you hurt?'

'No . . . no, I'm all right.'

She took Jason's proferred hand and he pulled her to her feet. Smoothing down her dress, she blushed, making sure the neckline of her dress was in place. 'I'm fine. I'd better be going.'

'You take care.' Tish patted her shoulder, and the couple returned to their cabin.

Taking a deep breath, Leda continued on her way, trying to ignore the shaking in her legs.

Leda paused when she emerged on deck and looked around. No one else was in sight at that moment, and the gentle swish of the sea as the ship cut through the Mediterranean created a calming atmosphere. Only the movement of the vessel caused a gentle breeze to caress her hair as the deck rocked gently under her feet. The air was still warm, and above her the moon was almost full, casting silver on the water.

Standing there for a few moments relaxed her and the unsettling incident outside the Rundles' cabin began to recede. She made her way round the deck, and was gratified to see a tall man silhouetted against the aft rail, looking out to sea.

As she approached, Nick heard her footfalls and turned, his face breaking into a welcoming smile. 'Leda, you came! I was beginning to think you'd turned in for the night.'

'No — but maybe I should have.'

As he took her hands, a frown creased his brow. 'Why? Has something happened? Is your aunt all right?' He led her to one of two chairs that were arranged at a little table.

'Aunt Ronnie is fine, just a little achy after all the walking in Rome. She's gone to bed.' As she laid her bag on the table, she put a hand to her knee, realising it was scraped from her sprawl on the carpet, and was now stinging.

She explained to Nick about the unseen person who had knocked her to the ground.

'But that's appalling that he didn't even stop to see how you were! Are you sure you want to stay? Would you rather return to your cabin?'

He took her hands in his, and as Leda looked into his eyes, she realised that was the last thing she wanted. A warm sensation was growing inside her at his genuine concern.

'No, I'm fine — a little shaken, and I have this scrape on my knee, but I'd rather relax here.'

Nick expressed dismay when she showed him her knee, but she assured him it didn't need any attention.

'Would you like some wine? Maybe that will help you to relax.' At her nod, he reached for the bottle of white wine that was sitting on a tray on the table, and poured a glass for each of them.

'I know it sounds strange, but I was sure that I saw two women coming out of the Rundles' cabin. But after I fell over, it was Jason who was with Tish. Do you think I might have imagined it?'

'Maybe it was a trick of the light — who knows?'

She sighed. 'You're right. I'm probably being fanciful. But I do find the Rundles an odd couple. I really can't take to them.'

He let her sip her drink for a while without interruption, and they sat in companionable silence. After a few minutes he said, 'Tell me about your day in Rome — did you enjoy it?'

Leda was thankful to talk about a different subject. 'Yes, we did. Aunt Ronnie was so thrilled to see the Sistine Chapel, though it was a hard, hot trek for her. I loved the sights, but wish we'd had time to get off the bus and explore properly.'

'You must go back, then.' He smiled.

The image, of him on the steps of St Peter's flooded her mind, and his conversation about hiding his identity. Realising her expression had changed by the responding frown on his face, she hurried on, 'You visited the Vatican, didn't you?'

He looked astonished, and, she thought, defensive. 'How do you know that?'

'Ronnie and I were in the Sistine Chapel and I thought I saw you. Then I caught a glimpse of you on the steps of St Peter's when I was rushing back to the bus.' She decided to push him further. 'You were on your mobile.'

He gave a wry smile. 'It seems I can't do anything without being found out. Yes, I went into Rome — it's one of the reasons I came on the cruise. I wanted to see the sights — St Peter's being one of them. I also visited the Colosseum, and wandered round the Roman Forum.'

Unwilling to spoil the atmosphere, she didn't tell him she'd overheard his conversation about concealing his identity. Maybe it was cowardly, but she was enjoying being with him.

'Very good material for a book by an

aspiring author, I imagine,' she commented mischievously.

His smile disappeared.

'No,' he said flatly, his voice curt.

Surprised at his defensive response, Leda challenged him. 'Surely you came on the cruise for the crime theme?'

There was a moody pause before he replied. 'I'm not interested in any lectures. I'd far rather talk about the ports of call. Are you going to Florence or Pisa tomorrow?'

Feeling he had deliberately avoided the question and diverted the conversation, Leda was tempted to probe further, but decided she didn't want to have an argument, and let it go.

'We have tickets for the bus to Florence. We're just going to make our own way round at our own pace. Auntie's not able to keep up with a walking tour. What about you?'

He laid his glass on the table. 'I haven't anything booked, but may take a train to the city.'

As they sat beneath the beautiful

141

moon, Leda became aware this was not what she had imagined for their evening together. Why were they talking about the ports of call, as if they were just acquaintances? Was that how Nick saw them? She looked into her glass and frowned.

'You look very fierce.'

'Do I? Maybe I'm wondering why you asked me here if it was just to chat about the sights.'

For a few moments he gazed intently into her face, then threw back his head and laughed.

'You mean, why did I choose a lovely moonlit night with wine, even without romantic music?'

Suddenly embarrassed, Leda put down her glass. 'I'd better go.' She stood up, but his hand caught her arm in a strong grip.

'Don't fly away, Leda. I'm sorry. I'm not much good at sweet nothings. I enjoy finding out about you. It's these everyday things that tell us about each other.'

Sitting again, she shook her head. 'But that's the whole point, Nick. You know little about me, and I know virtually nothing at all about you.'

'Why don't we change that? You start. Are you an only child? Where do your parents live?'

'I have a brother three years older called Adam — he's an architect. He lives in London, and he's married to Jenny, who's a science teacher in a secondary school. They don't have any children, although I think that may change soon. My parents live in Durham, not far from Aunt Ronnie.'

'And where do *you* live?'

'Newcastle — I bought a small house there a few years ago when I was working for a design company. Thankfully I can still keep up the payments with what I earn now.'

'You began your own business last year?'

'Yes, it's doing well . . . your turn . . .'

'Two older sisters, Ella and Julia. Ella is married with two children, Julia is

143

divorced. She has a son, fourteen now. They try to boss me about, but I escaped to the wilds of Derbyshire. My mother lives in Lancashire, in a world of her own — she's an academic, a university lecturer in history. My father was an archaeologist, but he died three years ago. He was caught in a rock fall while excavating in a cave.'

'I'm so sorry, Nick. Your mother must have been devastated.'

He stretched out his legs and leaned back in his chair, running one hand over his hair.

'Yes, we all miss him. He was eccentric, but caring. No matter where he was in the world, he kept in touch. I miss his crazy texts and emails.'

'And what about you?' she asked, softly. 'Have you ever been married?'

He looked out to sea for a moment.

'No, although I nearly was, a few years ago. It was just before Dad died. I was going to ask my girlfriend to marry me, but by the time the dust settled after we lost Dad, I found that I had lost the spark in the relationship. Shortly afterwards I moved to Derbyshire — and acquired my dog.'

'So there's no one in your life now?'

There, she had said it.

At that moment, the door behind them burst open, and a trail of laughing passengers doing a conga erupted on deck. The sound of a live band playing Latin American music accompanied them, as they skipped and hopped. A man reached for Leda and pulled her to her feet, holding her firmly so she couldn't resist. A woman behind them hauled Nick up, and they found themselves reluctantly caught up in the party. They danced round the deck a few times, then back into the lounge, where a band in colourful outfits played. The dance went on and on, until finally it came to a halt, the revellers cheering and clapping and shouting for more.

Some of the loudest calls came from the bar area, drawing Leda's attention. With a lurch, she saw it was the

Rundles. Tish was laughing, holding up a glass containing a brightly coloured cocktail, which she tipped into her mouth. Jason put two fingers to his lips and gave a loud whistle. Around them, other holidaymakers clapped.

Leda and Nick untangled themselves from the paper streamers that had become wound round them as they danced. Looking at the clock, she realised it was well past midnight. The moment and the mood had gone, she realised poignantly.

'I have to go. I need to be up early for our excursion in the morning.'

He nodded. Yet again he walked her back to her cabin, but this time he touched a finger to her chin and brushed her lips with his gently. It wasn't exactly a romantic kiss, but it set her pulses racing.

'Until tomorrow,' he murmured, and left her.

10

When she returned from her run the following morning, Leda found Ronnie sitting on the bed, examining her ankles.

'Oh, Leda, my ankles are still swollen, and my knees, too. I'm not going to be able to take the trip to Florence today.'

Leda sat beside her great aunt and put an arm round her shoulders. 'What a shame! I know you've been looking forward to it so much.'

Ronnie sighed. 'It's one of the penalties of growing older. I have to pace myself, and that was a heavy day yesterday.'

'Couldn't you just come on the bus and sit in a café all day?'

Ronnie shook her head wryly. 'I looked at the map they gave us with the information yesterday. We're to be dropped off at the station, and it's a fair walk into the centre.'

'I wonder if we can give the tickets to someone else. Maybe there's a waiting list?'

'No, no — you must go. It's too good an opportunity to miss.'

'But I couldn't go without you. If you're incapacitated, you need me here with you.'

Her aunt smiled. 'I'll be fine. I'll sit with a book in the shade on deck, or if that's too hot, in the lounge. The waiters are so attentive, I won't even need to get up for a drink. I'll have lunch in the restaurant, give myself a little treat to make up for not getting on the trip. I'm sure I'll find someone to talk to — everyone is so friendly.' At Leda's protest, she held up her hand and went on, 'I really think you should ask Nick to go with you — unless he's already booked on one of the buses.'

'No, he's not — but I don't know his cabin number. How do I contact him?'

'Ask the people at the information

desk to call for him over the loudspeakers. By the way, how did it go last night?' Her eyes twinkled.

Heat travelled up Leda's cheeks. 'It was nice. We sat on deck talking for a while, and the moon was so beautiful. But then we were caught up in a conga line and pulled into the party in the Sky Lounge, and it sort of dissipated the mood. I came back to the cabin after that.'

Ronnie burst out laughing at the tale of the conga. Then she shooed Leda off to the information desk to arrange the call for Nick.

* * *

The ship was docking at Livorno as a message was broadcast for Nicholas Drake to go to the information desk immediately. Leda sat on one of the seats by the window, watching for his arrival.

About ten minutes later, he appeared, his hair damp and standing on end, as if he had come straight from the shower. He was wearing beige chinos and an open-necked blue sport shirt. His face was blank with anxiety, and his eyebrows rose in consternation when he spied Leda.

'Leda, what is it? Are you all right?'

She came forward and put a hand on his arm in reassurance. 'It's all right, don't worry. Ronnie felt she overdid things yesterday in Rome, so she's decided to spend the day on board ship. But she wants you to use her ticket for the bus to Florence. Would you like that?'

'To go with you?' He ran a hand through his hair, making it stand up even more. 'That's very kind of her — of course, I'll pay for it. It won't cause any problems if I use it?'

'The tickets are both in my name because I ordered them, to be put on our cabin bill.'

'Are you sure you don't want to stay with her?'

'I offered, but she insists she's all

150

right. Her ankles *are* rather swollen, her knees, too — she suffers from arthritis — but she insists a day of rest on board will have her fighting fit for tomorrow. It's a much easier day, as we haven't booked anything, and can relax in the port. But today there wasn't any alternative to lots of walking.'

Finally persuaded, Nick agreed to accompany her. As Leda showed her identity card to the crew member at the exit, she admitted she was feeling a flutter of excitement at spending a day with Nick. Of course, it was sad for Ronnie that she would miss the splendours of Florence, especially when she had been looking forward to it. What's more, Nick might leave her once they reached the city. He might not want to be in her company all day.

As they stepped off the gangplank, Nick pulled a cotton hat from his pocket.

Her lips twitched in a smile. 'Are you really going to wear that?'

'Don't mock! Better to look silly than

suffer sunstroke. It's going to be another scorcher of a day. Anyway, I can't compete with this.' He flicked the wide brim of her sun hat, and she laughed.

Their guide on the bus was a bubbly young Italian woman with a pleasant sense of humour, and the trip to Florence passed quickly. In the distance, they caught a glimpse of the city of Pisa, complete with a shadowy silhouette of the renowned leaning tower, visible in the distance.

'Have you ever been to Pisa?' Nick asked.

'No — this is all new for me. What about you?'

'I'm like you. I've never been on a cruise before. I tend to go for treks to interesting places. Last year I spent a week in Iceland. We had some very cold bathing in one of the lakes!' He grinned.

She shivered theatrically. 'I like being active on holiday, but that's a bit extreme! I went to Germany with my friend Helena, and we explored some of the Rhine and Mosel region. I thought that would be my last fling for a while, what with starting the new business. So it's a surprise to find myself with Aunt Ronnie on this cruise. What's more, I wasn't expecting it to be so interesting.'

Although she'd said it with complete innocence, she felt a blush rising on her cheeks again, especially when he murmured, 'Neither did I.' He was looking straight into her eyes and she blinked and turned to look out of the window again, her breath tight in her chest.

They disembarked by the station at Florence. The guide had offered to walk the passengers from the bus drop-off point through to the Duomo, the famous cathedral of the city, situated right in the centre of the tourist area, and a good starting point for their exploration. Leda and Nick followed her and the other tourists. As they passed, the guide gave information about notable buildings.

'Good, isn't she?' Nick murmured as

they pressed on towards the Duomo.

Leda nodded. Gianetta was fluent in English, and had a lively manner when talking about the points of interest. She was also happy to answer questions.

When they reached the main square, the magnificent façade of the cathedral made Leda gasp. Its brilliant white and green marble provided a sharp contrast against the vibrant blue sky. Gianetta pointed out several important sights in the square, including the golden door of the St John Sacristy. Leda took a good number of photos, not just for herself, but also so she could show them to Ronnie later.

Nick took her smartphone and insisted on taking her photograph in front of the golden door. 'I'm sure your aunt will want to see pictures of you as well.'

Feeling self-conscious at his scrutiny, even through a camera lens, she smiled shyly.

At that moment, the guide called them over.

'If you would like, I will take you on this route.' She pointed to the tourist map they all carried, on which she had marked a red line to show the route through to the Piazza di Santa Croce. 'You will see many sights if you go this way, and I can tell you about them as we pass them.'

'What do you want to do?' Nick murmured.

Her mind working, Leda wavered. She wanted to time to explore the sights, not just gallop through on a tourist trail. She supposed she could buy a guide book at one of the myriad tourist stalls they passed. But it would be lovely to look at them in Nick's company. 'It sounds quite a good idea.'

His expression brightened at her response. 'I think it would be good to follow the guide, then we can branch off and do what we feel like.'

Her heart soared. He had said 'We' as if he was including her in his plans. Her face broke into a brilliant smile. 'Yes, let's do that.'

They did their best to cling to the group in the crowded streets, listening to the guide. Some attractions, like the bronze boar, were so crowded they agreed to come back later to try and see it better. Gianetta had told them people who stroked the bronze snout of the boar would return to Florence.

'I'd like to come back to the city, wouldn't you?' Nick said.

'Of course — we're just having a taste of it today, we couldn't possibly see everything,' she replied as they followed the guide.

They were also impressed by the reproduction of the statue of David by Michelangelo outside the Palazzo Vecchio. It was unlikely they would have time to visit the museum where the original was housed. By the time they reached the Piazza di Santa Croce, it was already past twelve o'clock, and Nick asked Gianetta for a recommendation for somewhere to eat. On their map, she pointed out a route through tiny streets to a restaurant she said had 'the best lasagne in Italy'.

When they reached the restaurant, they discovered some of the other people from their bus had also been directed to the same place. Judging by the wait for a table, the reputation of the restaurant was clearly excellent.

When they were ready to choose their food, they both opted for the lasagne Gianetta had recommended. It certainly looked delicious when the plates were laid in front of them. Taking a morsel on her fork to her mouth, Leda closed her eyes and savoured it.

'It's wonderful — it just melts on the tongue.'

She heard Nick laugh, and opened her eyes to glare at him. 'And just what is so funny?'

'You look as if you're in heaven — and all over a lasagne.'

'Don't you agree it's good?' Why did he tease her so?

He nodded, taking another forkful. 'You're right. I must try and lose myself in lasagne and experience heaven as well.' He shut his eyes, mimicking her expression.

She kicked him playfully under the table.

'Nicholas Drake, you are incorrigible. Stop it!'

He swallowed and grinned. 'Where to next?'

Feeling a glow of happiness at their ease with each other, she reached for the map.

'Definitely the Ponte Vecchio. I've seen pictures of all the shops crowded on the old bridge. Then we could wend our way back, taking more time at some of the places we passed with Gianetta. What do you think?'

He agreed. 'But first I think we should look at the church in the square, the one called the Basilica di Santa Croce. There are some famous tombs, like Rossini, Galileo and Machiavelli.'

'Tombs? Are you so immersed in crime that you need to look at tombs when you're on holiday?' She pulled a face.

'I think you'll find they're beautiful. Don't you like Renaissance churches?'

'I suppose so, but don't let's spend too long there. There's so much to see, and it's such a lovely sunny day.'

Once they were inside the church, Nick picked up a guide sheet in English and led her round, pointing out the beautiful sculptures. It was very peaceful and cool after the intense heat outside.

'There, that wasn't so bad, was it?' He looked at her with mischief in his eyes.

'I do like old churches, I'm just keen to see the Ponte Vecchio and don't want to leave it too late.'

Nick glanced at his watch. 'We still have three hours before we have to be back at the station. But you're right, we'd better make sure we see the sights we really want to.'

As they made their way back to the entrance, Leda decided there was also no time like the present to probe further.

'You mentioned you're not married, but you never did get to tell me if you had someone special waiting for you at home.' Her heart was beating faster, half frightened of his answer.

He turned to her, his face relaxed. 'No, there's no one waiting for me except my dog.'

She had to trust his reply. How could she judge otherwise? 'And what's your job like? I take it you're self-employed?'

'Yes, I'm self-employed.'

'So do you get many cases, as a freelance lawyer? Are you attached to a practice?'

He grabbed her hand and pulled her towards him, gazing deep into her eyes. 'So many questions! The answers would be too boring to imagine. This is far more interesting.' At that, he put his arms round her and drew her close so their bodies touched, and bent his lips to press them against hers.

Taken by surprise, she almost resisted, then with an explosion of sensation, realised this was all she wished for. Her body relaxed, as his lips took hers passionately. He pressed her tightly against him, so the whole length of them melded into each other.

As they parted to draw breath, she looked deep into his eyes, sighing. There were no words for what she was feeling, her pulse racing, her breath ragged and short. His hand stroked her hair, drawing her head on to his shoulder. They stood like this for a few moments, then she felt his voice resonating in his chest as he spoke.

'Much as I'd like to stay like this forever, we'd better make the most of our time here.'

She gave a shaky laugh, pulling apart to look into his face again. The intensity of his expression belied the casual words. He gave her a soft kiss on the lips. 'Are you ready to press on?'

'Of course,' she murmured.

They left the church hand in hand. It was a connection that felt so right. It felt blissful, laughing as they braved the crowds on the Ponte Vecchio. There wasn't time to browse the wonderful jewellery shops that crowded on the bridge, as they wanted to walk along the shore and look at the ancient backs of the shops.

After taking several photographs, they made their way back towards the Duomo. On the way they stopped to stroke the muzzle of the bronze boar, which was shiny with countless hands that had done the same. Leda took Nick's photo as he did so. Their eyes met, and she read in them that he wanted to return to Florence — with her.

Her breath caught. How could she feel so intensely about this man whom she had met such a short time ago?

The heat was searing as they walked along, hand in hand.

'Gelato?' Nick pulled her towards an ice cream parlour.

'Oh, yes, I'm melting!'

They went indoors, where it was cooler.

'There's nothing as good as an Italian ice cream,' she sighed, licking the cherry flavour, then the blackberry, that she had chosen.

'You look so intense, savouring the flavours.'

Surprised at his turn of phrase, she looked at him closely.

'For a dry lawyer, you have quite a way with words.'

'Maybe it's reading all those crime novels,' he grinned, licking his rum and raisin ice cream.

'Tell me more about Derbyshire . . .'

They spent longer than intended in the ice cream parlour, talking more about their homes and families. Leda began to relax, feeling she was breaking through the barriers Nick had built around his personal life.

'We'll have to hurry if we want to be back at the meeting point on time,' he finally said.

This time his arm was round her shoulders as he guided her through the hordes of people who thronged the streets, dodging those who had stopped to take pictures or look at the many souvenir stalls. Leda paused briefly to buy a guide book in English to take back for Ronnie.

They were on time for the rendezvous, and Leda spent much of the bus journey back to the ship looking through the guide book.

'There's so much to see in Florence — we only scratched the surface.'

'But it was good to experience what we did.'

They sat in companionable silence, hands intertwined, until the guide had everyone on the bus playing a game with Italian words. They descended to the quayside laughing.

Leda and Nick glanced briefly at two police cars waiting by the gangplank, but walked past, oblivious of the scrutiny of the policemen who stood by one of the cars. Once they had boarded the ship, they stood in the corridor, looking into each other's eyes.

'I'm going to have to dash off. We're

a bit late, and Ronnie will be waiting for me. I want to make sure she's all right. Besides, we'll need to change to be ready for the early sitting for dinner.'

'What are your plans for this evening? Are you going to the show again?'

'I'll see what Aunt Ronnie wants to do. She'll probably be glad of the entertainment if she's been alone all day.'

They made their way upstairs to the information area to check what was on that evening. To their surprise, they found Ronnie sitting having a cup of tea. She looked up and waved them over, her face full of concern.

'Did you see the police cars on the quayside? Have you heard the news?'

Mystified, they sat. Ronnie hadn't even noticed they had been holding hands.

'No. What's going on?' Nick said.

'It's the Rundles — more to the point, Tish Rundle. She's gone missing!'

11

Leda was utterly aghast. 'Gone missing! Where? In Florence?'

'No — apparently she disappeared from their cabin overnight. They've been searching for her all day without finding her.'

Nick looked shocked. 'This is really serious. How did you find out about it?'

Ronnie drained the last of her tea and pushed the cup to one side, leaning forward.

'Well, I took my time getting ready. After I'd sorted out what I needed, I took myself up to the Promenade Deck, where I read my book all morning, then took a little lunch in the shade beside the pool. I met Jackie and Steve again — remember the couple we sat with at the Captain's Dinner?' At Leda's murmur of agreement, she continued. 'It was quite hot by this time, so I decided to go to the Information desk to look for information about Florence. I had the idea that, even if I couldn't get to the city, I would imagine all the things you were doing.'

Leda grasped her aunt's hand and pressed it sympathetically.

'I was sitting here reading the leaflets, when I became aware of a commotion at the information desk. I realised it was Jason Rundle. He was so agitated, his voice raised as he was urging them to call his wife again over the ship's loudspeakers.

''But we've already called three times,' the young woman said. Then she said that as she hadn't responded, they'd have to report her as missing. 'She can't be, I don't understand it,' he kept saying, over and over, wringing his hands. It was quite distressing, seeing him so upset.

'I went over to the desk and asked him if there was anything I could do to help. 'Have you seen Tish today?' he asked me, rather pitifully I thought. He was on the verge of tears! He said she must have left their cabin during the night, and he haden't seen her since.

'He'd looked everywhere, and the ship had paged her, but she hadn't responded. He said he was told she might have gone with the buses into Florence, but that was totally ridiculous! The security people had no record of her leaving the ship, and everyone has to go the same way. In any case, why would she go ashore without telling him, he said, leaving their room while he was asleep? It did seem rather odd, I agreed, but all I could do was take his hands in sympathy.

'At that point the senior crew member for the information desk came to speak to Jason, asking him if he wanted to make a formal report that Tish was missing. He said the security staff on board would start an investigation, but as we were in an Italian port, they would have to inform the Italian police. The poor man just broke down! I felt so sorry for him. I asked if there was a private room where we could continue the discussion, and the steward took us into an office.

'Quite soon the senior security officer arrived — a nice young lady called Marika — and she began to question Jason.

'Apparently the couple had been partying until the small hours, and got back to their cabin at about two. Jason said he'd been drinking quite heavily and fell asleep immediately. He didn't wake until the ship was docking, and Tish wasn't in the cabin. He thought perhaps she had gone for breakfast, but he went to look for her and couldn't find her. He told me he'd been searching all morning, and couldn't find her anywhere — and she hadn't returned to the cabin.

'I stayed with Jason until the police arrived, about an hour ago. Then I left him with them, so they could question him in depth.'

Leda put her hands to her cheeks in shock.

'Do you think she really has disappeared — or has she just been ashore?'

Nick looked at the clock, which now read 5.50. 'We're due to set sail at six, but I expect they'll wait a while to see if she returns. But if she doesn't, they might have to consider that something more sinister has happened.'

'Such as what?' Leda looked apprehensive.

Nick's expression was grim. 'That she might have gone overboard during the night.'

The three of them sat in silence, Nick's words hanging in the air between them like a spectre.

After a few moments, Ronnie finally said, 'I wonder how long they'll wait here at Livorno? Maybe the ship will have to stay in port until they have done a thorough investigation — after all, we're heading for France overnight.'

'I suppose it will depend on whether they think she really did leave the ship, or something happened at sea,' Nick said, his expression serious. 'But it's such a difficult situation, with people coming and going all the time. They may just assume she went ashore without telling her husband and decided not to come back.'

Leda shook her head. 'So many different things could have happened. She might have gone ashore and been attacked, or kidnapped!'

'But why would she go ashore without her husband? They looked devoted,' Ronnie insisted. 'And I can assure you he was very upset.'

'Cruise ships are very strict counting people off and on. Anyone entering or leaving the vessel has to show identification,' Nick pointed out. 'Unless someone has been lax, there's no way she could disembark without record of it. We'll just have to wait and see. Are you going into dinner as usual?'

Leda looked confused. 'I . . . I don't know. It seems callous, to go on as if nothing happened.'

Ronnie took her hand. 'Maybe we should just go as usual. I won't feel like

171

dressing up, but at least we should eat. What do you think, Nick?'

'I don't see any problem. I eat in the cafeteria as it means I can be more flexible, and I don't like dressing up anyway. I expect the cruise company will want to keep this as low-key as possible. It's not something they'll want to advertise.'

★   ★   ★

Leda and Ronnie sat at their usual dining table, picking at their food, conscious the whole time of the two empty places opposite them.

'I can't say I particularly liked Tish, but this is such a terrible thing to happen, I wouldn't wish it on anyone,' Leda said in a low voice when she finally put down her dessert spoon.

At that moment, her heart leapt into her mouth as a policeman approached their table.

'Signora Denham, Signorina Hollings — you usually share this table with

Signor Rundle and his wife?'

'Yes, that's right,' Ronnie said.

'When you are finished your meal, please would you come to the information desk, as we wish to ask you some questions. You have heard that Signora Rundle is reported missing?'

'Yes, my aunt has spoken with Mr Rundle. We're finished eating, aren't we, Aunt Ronnie? We can go with you now.'

They left the restaurant in the company of the police, feeling all eyes on them. Leda wondered how many on board knew about the drama. Of course, they would be aware the ship hadn't set sail on time, and the police were on board.

The two women were questioned together, which made Leda feel better. She had never been involved in a police investigation before, and had horror pictures in her mind of the sort of thing she'd seen in TV dramas, and she didn't want Aunt Ronnie disturbed by intense interrogation.

She had expressed this to her aunt on their way to the information desk.

'Don't worry about me,' Ronnie declared. 'I won't let anyone intimidate me. Besides, we have nothing to hide. Just remember that, my dear.'

'But you've not been well today.'

Ronnie gave an exclamation of denial. 'I wasn't ill — just not mobile. In any case, my ankles are fine, now. Plenty of rest this morning made all the difference. I missed going to Florence, but it was the sensible thing to do.'

In the interview room, which was the office of the chief security officer, they were invited to sit, with a policeman opposite them. He spoke impressively good English.

'We hardly knew the Rundles, really,' Ronnie explained. 'We only met them for the first time at the start of the cruise, when they joined us at our dinner table. We didn't socialise with them.'

'Originally they were seated with another couple, Jackie and Steve from

Glasgow. We don't know their sur-name,' Leda added. 'The Rundles asked to move to sit by the window.'

The policeman nodded. 'When did you last see them?'

'We had dinner as usual after the visit to Rome, didn't we, Auntie? That was yesterday.'

'Did they seem any different? Agitated, or worried perhaps?'

'They were always full of stories about their day,' Ronnie told the policeman. 'They had been to Rome, and taken one of the tours. But they did like sunbathing. They told us that was what they were planning for today, as they didn't like sightseeing every day.'

'I saw them again after dinner,' Leda put in. 'I was with a friend on deck much later in the evening, and we were pulled into the party in the Rio Lounge. The Rundles were at the bar, but they weren't taking part in the dancing. Maybe the barman could tell you more.'

The policeman made a note, then

asked, 'What time was this?'

'About half past eleven.'

'And the name of your companion?'

She blushed at the term. It sounded so intimate. 'Nicholas Drake.'

The policeman asked a few more minor questions about their background, then released them with his thanks.

'I wonder how Jason is?' Ronnie said as they made their way back to their cabin. 'Shall we call on him, do you think?'

Leda frowned. 'I would have thought the police would be looking after him.'

'But he's all alone. Shall we consult with Nick?'

There hadn't even been time to tell Ronnie about their day in Florence. Leda sighed. 'I just feel so confused. Here we are on a cruise that may have come to a halt. Tish is missing, and the horror is that she could have drowned. I just don't know what we should do!'

'Well, I think we should change into

176

something more comfortable and get a cup of tea.'

Leda smiled. It was Ronnie's answer to everything — a cup of tea — but she agreed it would be a good starting point. They didn't want to be skulking in their cabin. It was just too small to inhabit for any length of time.

The entertainment was going on as scheduled. Strains of singing drifted out of the Hollywood Lounge as they passed, where there was a show of seventies hits. Leda wasn't tempted this evening, as she couldn't have faced sitting still. All these people who had no connection with the trouble had no problem switching off.

Arms linked, the two women strolled round the deck in the dusk. Then, to her delight, Leda spotted Nick leaning against the rail, looking down at the port. He turned as they approached.

'Leda, Ronnie . . . are you both all right? I called at your cabin earlier, but you weren't there.'

He pulled up a chair for Aunt

177

Ronnie, while Leda leaned against the rail with him.

'We were questioned by the police. They want to talk to you, too.'

'Yes, they found me, and I've been grilled. I had to admit I didn't even recognise the Rundles in the bar, as I've never met them. You didn't particularly care for them, did you?'

Leda shook her head. 'I feel a bit guilty about that. We were wondering about looking for Jason to see if he needed support. They didn't seem to have made friends with anyone on board.'

'I'll come with you, if you like. He might like another man to talk to.'

12

Leda was able to remember the location of the Rundles' cabin. She was quite surprised to discover it was directly above theirs. Nick knocked on the door, but though they waited then tried again, there was no reply.

'Let's leave a note,' Ronnie said, delving into her handbag. She scribbled on a little pad, tore off the page and folded it, and Nick slid it under the door. 'At least he knows we care and we're there for him if he needs us.'

'What do you want to do now?' Nick asked as they headed back towards the lifts.

'There's a piano player in the New York Lounge from eight o'clock until ten. Maybe we should get a cup of coffee and sit there,' Leda suggested.

'That sounds ideal,' Ronnie agreed.

There were quite a few other people

in the small lounge, and the woman singer had a pleasant voice. Her repertoire was a mixture of jazz classics and easy listening songs, which were relaxing to listen to and unobtrusive in the background.

Leda decided it would be a good idea to tell Ronnie about their day in Florence, to take their minds off Tish's disappearance. However, she didn't mention anything about their kiss in the church — how could she, with Nick sitting there?

She was aware of his eyes on her as she mentioned the Basilica di Santa Croce and the famous tombs, which had Ronnie's eyes popping with delight.

'Imagine, all those famous people buried there! I had no idea. Well, I shall certainly book another cruise next year to come back here. I shall save myself for a visit to Florence.'

'I'm sure Mum would love to come. She was so disappointed at missing this holiday.'

'Have you spoken to her this week?

How is she? It was very unfortunate she broke her wrist.'

Leda said she'd phoned her mother that morning when they were in port, and was well.

'Of course, she's very envious of all we're experiencing. She sent her love, and was sorry to hear you had to miss today's trip.'

Leda hadn't mentioned to her mother that she was taking a very attractive man with her to Florence instead of Aunt Ronnie. That would have sparked huge interest from her mother, who would have wanted updates on the situation every few hours! Leda couldn't be sure if her time with Nick was any more than just a holiday fling, and didn't want her mother getting any ideas.

Nick joined in with some of the descriptions, which pleased Leda. He didn't seem to want to leave them and pursue his own interests. It was gratifying that he was happy in the company of an elderly woman, just as easy with her as he was with people his own age. Ronnie was half flirting with him, too, Leda surmised with a mental chuckle. It was good for her great aunt to be in the company of younger people. Soon they were exchanging ideas about their favourite authors.

'I'm really enjoying the latest Harry Agnew. Are you a fan of his?'

Nick's expression was thoughtful. 'Well, I am familiar with his books . . .'

'So you've read a few? Do you like his style?'

'I think he has promise.'

'Promise! He's a best-selling author, which I would say fulfils his promise!'

Nick laughed. 'Yes, but he's got some way to go before he reaches the heights of the great authors like Agatha Christie, P D James and Ruth Rendell. Come to think of it, they're all women. Do you think women are better at crime fiction?'

They were off again. Leda sat back, looking out of the window. It was almost ten o'clock, and they were still in port. Yet again her mind strayed to the problem of Tish Rundle . . .

How could she have just disappeared? Didn't the cruise ship have CCTV cameras everywhere? If she had gone overboard, surely it would be on camera? If she had slipped ashore, how would she have managed to get past the strict security? Everyone had to show their identity card as they disembarked and boarded again, even the crew.

But why would she want to run away from her husband? Was there something sinister in their relationship that she and Ronnie hadn't fathomed? They seemed so much in harmony, enjoying their cruise. Though of course, there were sometimes some furtive exchanges between the two. What had they been about?

At about quarter past ten, Ronnie declared herself thoroughly exhausted by the day's events.

'I'm off to bed now. If we make it to Villefranche tomorrow, I'd like to be able to go ashore. We had wondered about going to Nice, which would be lovely. You two stay a bit longer.'

Leda kissed her cheek and asked if she would like an arm to help her back to the cabin. Ronnie assured her she would be fine, and left the two of them together.

Nick's face was gentle as he looked at her. 'You looked miles away, there. What were you thinking about?'

Leda shook her head. 'I'm afraid I can't get this business of Tish Rundle out of my head.' She told him about what had been going through her mind.

'You'd be surprised how much can slip through the security net,' he told her. 'There will be a few blank spots in the security camera system, for sure. Then there's the possibility she got ashore with an accomplice on the crew who let her through without scanning her card.'

'Do you think the police will question everyone on board?'

'I don't know. It's a tall order. I suppose it depends on how much

184

responsibility the Italian police feel they owe to the case. After all, if she disappeared overboard, they could consider it an international incident, and just close it at that.'

At that moment, Nick's mobile phone rang. Lifting it from his pocket, he looked at the caller's identity, and sighed. 'I have to take this, if you don't mind. Excuse me for a moment.'

He put it to his ear as he jumped to his feet, walking quickly from the lounge. Leda heard him say, 'Hello — yes, it's Nick. Are you sorted out?' before he disappeared out of earshot.

She wondered if he was leaving because of the background noise, or whether it was something he didn't want her to hear. It was rather late in the evening for a call. He was gone about ten minutes. She could see him through the glass door at the entrance to the lounge, gesticulating again like he had been in Rome, when she'd seen him on the phone.

'Sorry about that,' he said on his

return, but didn't tell her who it was. Was she being paranoid, thinking he was being secretive?

The singer had finished her set some time ago, and when Leda looked at her watch it was almost eleven o'clock. Weariness washed over her. It had been such a strange day. Much as she wanted to stay in Nick's company, she declined when he offered to take her to the Jazz Lounge again. They parted at the lifts, exchanging a quick brush of the lips.

In the cabin, Ronnie was already asleep, and Leda didn't delay in climbing into her own bed. Despite the stimulating events of the day, she quickly drifted into sleep.

Later in the night she roused briefly, and became aware that the ship was moving. They had left Livorno and were on their way to France.

* * *

Leda woke at her usual time, the sun gilding the porthole. The ship was stationary, the blue sea and sky a vision of tranquillity. For a moment she was only aware of the beauty of the early morning, then the events of the previous day burst into her memory and she sat up with a start.

Ronnie was sitting up in bed, reading. She pushed her glasses down her nose, looking at Leda. 'Did you sleep well, dear? We docked about twenty minutes ago.'

'How could I have slept so deeply with all that going on?'

Ronnie laid down her book. 'We've arrived in France, I believe. It seems the Italian police have let us go.'

'I wonder what their decision was.' Leda swung her legs out of bed and stood up, stretching.

'I've been thinking about that. There are various possibilities . . . they could have found Tish, or they could have decided she definitely went overboard, and that their investigations were fruitless. Or they may have decided to pass the investigation onto another authority.'

'I hope she's turned up. Still, I suppose we'd better get on with the day. I'll go for my run as usual, if you don't mind. I need to clear away some cobwebs.'

As her feet pounded the deck, Leda began to relax, and it was with a lift of her heart that she noticed Nick at the bow rail as she completed her third circuit of the deck.

He turned to her with a smile. 'I hoped you'd be out here for your run. How did you sleep?'

Coming to a halt beside him, she wiped a hand over her brow, dewed with perspiration. It was going to be another warm day. 'Surprisingly well. Have you heard any news about Tish Rundle?'

He leaned back against the rail, the sun glinting off his bronzed arms, the sight of which made Leda's heart flip.

'No, but I suppose I could ask at the information desk. Presumably the cruise is proceeding as normal, but why the ship was released, I have no idea. And I haven't seen any sign of Jason Rundle, either.'

As they walked back to the door, Leda glanced at her watch. It was time to accompany her aunt to breakfast. 'What are your plans for today? Have you booked a trip to Nice or Monaco?'

He looked up towards the bleached houses of Villefranche, nestling in the shelter of the steep cliffs of the French Riviera.

'No, I need to be free today. There's something I have to do later. It would be good to look around Villefranche, but I have no idea if I'll manage it.'

Her heart sank. The fact that he didn't meet her eyes disturbed her. She had been hoping she would be able to spend more time with Nick. Still, she had to make it up to Ronnie for missing the Florence trip.

'We didn't book anything, either,' she replied as coolly as she could, covering up her disappointment. 'I expect we'll go ashore and take a train to Nice. The information sheet says it doesn't take long.'

'Well, I must go. If you find out anything about Jason or Tish, let me know. This is my cabin number, and my mobile phone number.' He scribbled it on a piece of paper and held it out.

Feeling dismissed and flat, Leda took the paper, thrusting it into her pocket. 'See you later, then,' she said, and hurried back inside. There was no way she would let him get to her!

★　★　★

After breakfast, Ronnie declared they ought to make an effort to find Jason and offer their support. 'After all, it looks as if we're the only people on board they talked to.'

Leda felt rather uncomfortable about this, not wanting to intrude, but once Ronnie had made up her mind, there was little she could do to dissuade her. They went straight from the breakfast table to Jason's cabin. To Leda's surprise, he answered their knock promptly.

'Jason, how are you?' Ronnie greeted him with a sympathetic expression. 'We wanted to let you know we're here for you if you want someone to talk to.' Her great aunt always seemed to know exactly what to say in a difficult situation.

Jason was dressed in a T-shirt and shorts, though his hair was unkempt and his eyes heavy as if he had not slept. For a moment his expression was defensive, but then he relaxed.

'That's very kind of you, Ronnie — and Leda. The Italian police are doing a helicopter search over the direction taken by the ship that night. It's really futile, I know — it's well known that if someone goes overboard, it's virtually impossible to find them ... ' He wiped his hands over his face, blinked and continued, 'There's a team flying out from England today to continue the investigation. They'll probably want to talk to you again.'

191

'Would you like to come for a coffee with us? It must be distressing for you, alone with your thoughts in the cabin.' Leda was surprised to find herself offering him company, because she still couldn't find it in herself to like Jason.

For a moment he looked undecided, then he nodded. 'Just let me grab a few things. I'll meet you on the Promenade deck in fifteen minutes.'

Leda and Ronnie returned to their cabin to get their hats and sunglasses, then made their way to the place he had suggested. They were surprised to find him at a table under an umbrella, with a laptop already set up. When they sat down, the waiter approached and they all ordered coffees.

At that moment, Leda became aware of Nick behind her.

'I hope you don't mind if I join you.' He held out a hand to Jason, introducing himself. 'I'm Nick Drake. I was on deck with Leda the night your wife went missing.'

Jason looked at him with narrowed

eyes, then relented and took his hand, nodding. 'I remember seeing you in the Latin Bar.'

Leda felt happier with Nick's support, and began to relax. It seemed he wasn't avoiding her company after all. He pulled up a chair, and placed the coffee cup he had been carrying on the table. The waiter brought the three drinks they had ordered, then Jason swivelled round the laptop so that they could see what was on it.

'The ship gave me a copy of the CCTV footage, from the night Tish disappeared. Look . . . this is just after 3am.'

They crowded round, seeing the black and white image of the Promenade deck. Within a few moments, the figure of a woman went past the camera. Leda gasped.

'Yes, that's Tish,' Jason said. 'Now . . . this is the next camera.'

At this point, Tish could be seen standing at the rail, looking down at the sea. Ronnie felt for Leda's hand, squeezing it hard. They didn't know what to expect — were they going to see her go over the side? But instead the woman on the screen moved out of the range of the camera within a few moments.

'This is the camera further along the deck — there are no more in between.'

The timeline followed on immediately from the previous one, but there was no one in the shot. Several minutes went by and still it stayed blank.

'So she disappeared somewhere between the last two camera shots?' Nick studied the screen.

Jason sat back, closing his eyes.

'I've been over and over all the footage with them, but she never appears again, not even in any of the other cameras on the deck. That's the last we ever saw of her.' His voice broke, and he put his head in his hands. Ronnie reached over and rubbed his arm sympathetically.

'Couldn't she just have slipped back

194

inside at one of the doors?' Leda surmised.

'There are cameras at most of the doors. We haven't been able to find any trace of her returning inside the ship. It's not irrefutable evidence, but the company security staff and the Italian police believe it's a good indication that she must have gone overboard.' Yet again his voice cracked, and he put his hands over his eyes, stifling a sob.

'I thought the British police were sending investigators?' Nick turned the laptop towards him and ran through the footage once more.

Jason sighed. 'I believe it's just a formality, as this is a British cruise ship. Now the Italian police have released us and the ship was allowed to continue to France, it looks as if they've come to the conclusion this was what happened. It's probably too late to find any evidence in the sea. I just can't believe it . . . my darling Tish. How could it have happened?'

Ronnie reached out a hand and

touched his arm. 'Maybe she wasn't feeling well and went out for some air. Perhaps she fainted.'

Jason placed his own hand over hers and looked into her eyes. 'If only I'd been there with her. Why didn't she tell me?' He shook his head. After a few moments of silence, he wiped his eyes. 'The ship's security staff are going to interview all the crew today, to see if anyone either saw her or may have helped her ashore. If only they find something . . . I must keep hoping.'

'Of course you must!' Leda exclaimed. 'You must find out the truth — and if there's any hope she's still alive, then you must find her.'

Jason nodded and closed up the laptop. All of a sudden he seemed to want to be alone, his face closing down. The others picked up on this, and made their farewells.

13

They walked further round the Promenade deck and found another table that was free. 'What do you think about that?' Ronnie asked Nick as they took their seats.

He turned to look at her with raised eyebrows. 'You don't believe it rings true?'

Ronnie shrugged. 'I'm sorry for him, but how could such a thing have happened? Why would Tish have left him in the middle of the night?'

Nick folded his arms, looking out to sea. 'Who knows? You said they were a strange couple.'

'Yes — but it's more that they were a bit defensive, veering between friendliness towards us and then the next minute making us feel uncomfortable. I couldn't make them out,' Leda said. 'But I always had the impression they were devoted to each other.'

Ronnie nodded. 'They were indeed. Oh, dear, this is such a terrible business! How can we enjoy the cruise with this hanging over us?'

Leda took her hand. 'Ronnie, we can't let this spoil the cruise. You've been looking forward to it for such a long time. Come on, I think we should make the effort to go ashore. What about you, Nick?' She looked at him, hoping he might have changed his mind — it would be lovely to have his company, even with Ronnie as chaperone.

He shook his head. 'I'm afraid not. Maybe I'll see you later this afternoon. You go ahead, and have a good day.'

They were taken ashore by tender as the ship was anchored in the bay and there wasn't a quay large enough for a cruise ship. Two other ships were anchored further out, larger vessels whose tenders zipped past at regular intervals. Earlier the places on the small boats from the Ocean Star had been required for those passengers who had booked on the bus trips to Monaco and Nice. Now these had departed and the tenders were free for the rest of the passengers who wanted to go ashore.

They tried to put Tish's disappearance to the back of their minds as they climbed into the boat. Leda held firmly onto Ronnie as she stepped off the gangplank, making sure her great aunt wouldn't trip or stumble. Soon they were bobbing in towards the shore.

'How quaint and attractive Villefranche is,' Ronnie commented as they approached the quayside. Old buildings in fondant shades of pink, peach, and yellow crowded round the little port. They were overlooked from the hills by modern white villas of the rich and famous. The heat wasn't so intense as in Rome or Florence. It felt just pleasantly warm as they stepped ashore.

Walking through the port entrance, they emerged on a crowded front street lined with cafés. Immediately opposite was a little market selling local goods, clearly aimed at tourists, and they couldn't resist taking a look. A pleasant half hour was spent browsing through lace goods, handbags, local produce, and the inevitable souvenir stalls. They came away with a few items, satisfied they had gifts for family and friends.

They decided to hop on the tourist train that trundled by road around the area of the fort, taking them up to a height where they could see the ships in the bay, including the Ocean Star, which looked dwarfed by the two giant cruise ships anchored nearby. A recorded commentary in several languages from the speakers of the little train gave them a potted history of the town. By the time they returned to the starting point, it was already midday.

★ ★ ★

They were reading a menu outside one of the cafés on the waterfront, when they realised someone was trying to attract their attention.

'Look, Leda — isn't that the nice couple we sat with at the Captain's Dinner?' Ronnie said.

Leda shaded her eyes and peered at the tables along the waterfront, from which two people were waving at them. 'Yes, that's Jackie and Steve. It looks as if they want us to join them.'

'I'd be quite happy to. The menu here looks good. Why not?'

The couple were sitting at a table laid for four people, and they beamed with delight as Leda and Ronnie came towards them.

'Not visiting Nice and Monaco?' Steve asked as he pulled out one of the empty chairs for Ronnie to sit.

'We thought we'd have a quieter day, with no scheduled tours. Villefranche is so pretty.'

Ronnie balanced her stick against the wrought iron fence which separated the outdoor dining area from the pavement. It was gently shaded by large yellow sun umbrellas. The restaurant building was on the other side of the pavement, which meant they were sitting on the side next to the harbour.

'What a wonderful setting,' Leda commented as she picked up the menu on the table to make her choice.

Once the waiter had taken their order, they relaxed into conversation. Inevitably the conundrum of Tish Rundle's disappearance came up. The reason for the disruption to the cruise schedule had spread quickly round the passengers.

Jackie pushed up her sunglasses until they sat on top her red-tinted hair. 'In all our years of cruising, we've never had anything like that happen. We were so shocked when we heard.'

Leda and Ronnie agreed, but Steve's expression was sceptical. He took a mouthful of his white wine and set his glass back on the table, fingering the stem thoughtfully.

'There's something really odd about the whole situation. Why is there no record of her going overboard? And the ship's riddled with security cameras, so if she didn't go overboard, how did she manage to avoid them all? If she's hiding somewhere, she must have an accomplice on the crew.'

Jackie laughed, and lifted her own glass.

'He can't switch off, even on holiday — always the investigator.'

Leda recalled that Steve was a researcher for an investigative TV show. 'Well, there's a team from Britain on it now,' she pointed out.

Jackie looked up as the waiter put an omelette with salad in front of her. She picked up her knife and fork. 'Let's forget about mysteries and enjoy this fabulous food. Look, yours is coming too.'

All four meals in place, they pushed away thoughts of the Rundles and began to talk of other matters. Soon they were enjoying their wine and food, and the mood lifted perceptibly. It was an enjoyable lunch with plenty of laughter, while they gazed at the boats in the harbour and the Ocean Star at anchor in the bay, and holidaymakers strolling past in shorts and sun hats. On one side of the café, traffic made its way through, on the other, people walked along the promenade. Tenders came into port regularly from the cruise ships anchored in the bay, disembarking passengers and taking others back.

Once they had finished their meal and settled the bill, Jackie asked what they were planning for the rest of the afternoon.

Leda turned to her great aunt.

'We've no particular plans. Would you like to wander round the town, Auntie?'

'Yes, I would. It's much cooler here than in Italy. As long as we take our time, I'd like to explore some of the little streets and buildings. And there's a church further up the hill, if I can make it up there.'

Jackie and Steve intended to return to the ship to do some more sunbathing.

'We've been here twice before, and

done the Nice and Monaco trips, so we just want to chill out,' Steve told them as they took their leave. With a wave, they headed back to the embarkation point for the tender to the Ocean Star.

Leda and Ronnie wandered the streets, taking in the colour-washed buildings with their wrought iron balconies overflowing with greenery. Leda wondered what it would be like to live all year round in a place with such a balmy climate. She daydreamed of summers when the sun shone every day, and where one could eat croissants and drink coffee on the balcony each morning. The thought was blissful!

Steps ran up steeply from the shoreline. Following these, they were soon immersed in the lanes of the town, dappled with sun and shade. They browsed attractive boutiques and themed shops. Eventually they reached the height of the yellow-washed church. It was open, and they were able to look inside, to Ronnie's delight.

When they emerged, they walked back down, using the wrought iron handrails frequently, as the way was steep. They paused to buy ice creams at one of the parlours on the way back to the port. Although it was just a ten-minute journey to Nice by train, they discovered it was a fair walk to the train station, so were satisfied it had been the right decision not to go there today.

By this time it was mid-afternoon. Ronnie declared she'd had a wonderful day, but would appreciate returning to the ship for a little siesta.

'Do you want to stay and do some more exploring?' she asked Leda.

'No, I'll come back with you. I might try and find a free sunbed on deck and read my book.'

★ ★ ★

They didn't have long to wait for the tender. As they climbed on board, they noticed a pretty young blonde woman hurrying towards the boat, wheeling a suitcase.

'Is this the tender for the Ocean Star?' she asked the crewman who was about to untie the rope to cast off. At his affirmative, she took his proffered hand and climbed on board, which proved to be a difficult manoeuvre in a short, tight skirt and high heels. He lifted her case in behind her, and she settled in one of the few remaining spaces at the other end of the boat.

Leda thought nothing more of her until they had crossed over to the Ocean Star and it was time to disembark. The newcomer was one of the first to leave the tender, pushing her suitcase ahead of her, causing a jam of people behind her. Leda felt she ought to have waited until most of the others had stepped off, so there would have been more space. But her attention was occupied with Ronnie's safety until they were both on the pontoon ready to embark on the ship once more.

They had shown their identity cards

and were entering the lobby to take the lift to their cabin, when Leda saw the newcomer ahead of them.

To her shock and surprise, she heard her saying, 'Nick, darling!' and saw her fling her arms round Nick Drake, who must have been waiting for her.

Leda stopped short, not wanting to be seen, and grabbed Ronnie's arm. Ronnie looked round in alarm, not having seen the greeting. But Nick and the young woman had disappeared into the lift, and Leda breathed a sigh of relief.

Nevertheless, her heart was pounding, and a pang of disappointment seared through her.

Why had Nick greeted this pretty young woman so enthusiastically, when he'd told her he didn't have anyone in his life? She was too young to be one of his older sisters.

Clearly, he must have been lying.

14

When they reached their cabin, Ronnie looked at her quizzically. 'You've gone very quiet. Are you feeling all right?'

With a sigh, Leda sat on the bed, throwing her bag down disconsolately. She decided to confide in her great aunt. 'Did you see that young woman with the suitcase who got on at the port?'

Ronnie loosened her sandals and kicked them off. 'I couldn't miss her — she made such a fuss! One of these confident types who thinks the world revolves around her.'

'I don't know if you saw who met her when we came on board . . . '

Ronnie looked mystified. 'Don't tell me she's one of the investigation team from Britain?'

Leda frowned. 'I doubt it — she met Nicholas Drake, and they embraced each other very warmly. She even called him 'darling', I heard it distinctly.'

Ronnie reached over and patted her hand.

'Don't get wound up too soon. There could be all sorts of stories behind who she is. Didn't you say he had two sisters?'

Leda leaned back, hands behind her head. 'Yes, but they're older than him. She's definitely younger, and looks nothing like him, no family resemblance at all.'

Ronnie gave a huge yawn. 'Pardon me. I'm going to have to shut my eyes for a while.' She looked across at Leda. 'Don't be too inventive. Nick doesn't seem the deceptive type to me. I can see how much he likes you, Leda. Why not go for a swim to cool off and relax?'

'You're right, a swim will be just the job. You have your rest, Auntie, and I'll be back later.'

She looked out her swimsuit, changed into it and wrapped a sarong skirt around her waist. Taking a tunic top and towel, she slipped on her sunglasses and hat, before leaving Ronnie.

★   ★   ★

The gentle sound of lapping water met her when she stepped out on the pool deck. There were three other people in the pool, one swimming up and down, the other two floating in the water enjoying the coolness. Leda quickly loosened her skirt and left it with her towel and other clothes on a nearby free sun lounger. She twisted her hair into a knot, before climbing down the steps into the small pool.

The water was blissfully cool, though not as icy as that first day, she mused. At the memory, her eyes quickly surveyed the surrounding area, almost expecting to see Nick, but there was no sign of him.

Pushing off from the side, Leda began a slow, leisurely breaststroke, revelling in the refreshing water lapping on her skin.

Leda spent about twenty minutes in the pool, taking her time and not exercising hard. Finally she climbed out, loosening her hair from the band as she stood under the shower beside the pool.

It was too soon to return to the cabin. Her aunt liked about an hour for her siesta, Leda had learned over the past few days. Draping her towel over the sun lounger, she stretched out to let the sun dry her body.

After a while, she decided she could do with quenching her thirst, so she tied on her sarong and went to the bar. She chose a long fruity drink, and was sipping it in the shade beside the bar when she caught sight of a woman walking on the deck above. Surely it was Tish Rundle!

Setting her glass on the bar, Leda hurried up the stairs. Seeing the blonde woman ahead of her, she covered the space between them, grasping the woman's arm. 'Tish!'

The woman swung round, pushing

her sunglasses up on to the top of her head. The heavily mascaraed eyes blinked at Leda in the bright sunlight — they were not Tish Rundle's.

'I'm sorry . . . I thought you were . . . sorry.'

She let her hand fall. The resemblance was uncanny, but it was not Tish. The woman shrugged, and pulled away, continuing on her way.

Feeling rather foolish, Leda returned more slowly down the steps to the bar and retrieved her drink. The calm she had achieved from her swim had deserted her, replaced by the dilemma of Tish's disappearance playing over in her thoughts.

Leda surmised she must have an overactive imagination, seeing the missing woman in the person of a stranger. She wondered if Jason was finding the same thing. What it would be like to lose someone dear to you in such a fashion, she could only imagine!

Finishing her drink, she thought again about Nick and the young blonde woman who had arrived on the tender. Though she agreed in principle with Ronnie's suggestion that there could be other explanations for the enthusiastic greeting, the warmth of it told her this was someone close to him — and probably romantically.

She would have loved to tell Nick about the woman who looked so like Tish. His cabin number was engraved on her memory. Could she risk going to find him? After all, if the young blonde was special to Nick, she could find them in a compromising position — and that would not just make her embarrassed, but be a knife in her heart.

She still had time to fill, so, going back to the pool, she retrieved her towel and pulled the skirt on over her swimsuit. Her hair had dried, so she combed it out until it hung in an ebony sheet down her back.

Nick's cabin was on the next deck down, so she soon reached the door. She paused outside, wondering if she would hear any sound through the door that would warn her if it was not safe to knock. Her heart was pounding. After a few moments, she gritted her teeth and rapped her knuckles on the door.

There was no response and she was about to leave, thinking he wasn't there. But then the door was flung open, to reveal Nick, his hair rumpled. Leda felt a pang of embarrassment and shock, seeing the young woman sitting on Nick's bed.

'I . . . I'm sorry, I didn't mean to disturb you. I can see you're occupied . . . ' Feeling hot blood suffuse her cheeks, she turned to flee.

Nick's hand flew out to catch her wrist and restrain her. 'No, don't go, Leda. You're not disturbing us. Come in.'

Immensely reluctant, she allowed herself to be pulled into the cabin. The young blonde woman looked up at her, eyes guileless. It was only then that Leda realised she was still in the dress she'd been wearing on the tender. There were files and papers spread out on the bed and the woman held one in her hands.

'Leda, this is Sophie — my agent's assistant.'

Confused, Leda looked from one to the other. Were they not involved after all? They had looked so comfortable when they greeted each other. Then, realising she had not responded, she quickly said, 'Pleased to meet you, Sophie.' She turned to Nick. 'What kind of agent? I thought you were supposed to be a freelance lawyer.'

'You mean you don't know who he really is?' Sophie gave a disbelieving laugh.

Nick silenced her. 'Not now, Sophie.'

A flicker of annoyance at his deception knotted Leda's insides. Then the significance of the word 'agent' struck her. 'You're a writer, aren't you?'

He spread his hands in defence. 'I'm sorry, Leda. I didn't mean to deceive you. There was a reason for keeping quiet. I'd like to explain it all to you, but Sophie and I have to get through some work now. Can I meet you later?'

Feeling aggrieved, Leda was about to say *Forget it!* but she looked at Sophie's polished, pretty face and realised her every move was being scrutinised. Not wanting to appear petty, she shrugged, trying to maintain her dignity.

'If you like. I expect I'll be taking Aunt Ronnie for afternoon tea later, or we could meet after dinner if that would be preferable.'

'After dinner — say about eight o'clock? Will your aunt want to see the show?'

'I don't know.' She found it hard not to snap at him for his irritating calmness. 'Make it quarter to eight outside the Hollywood Lounge. If Auntie wants to see the show we can leave her there.'

He followed her to the door of the cabin.

'Until later — I'm truly sorry, Leda.' His eyes pleaded with her, but she was in no mood for clemency. He had been underhand; it galled her.

'See you later,' she replied curtly, and turned smartly on her heel to stalk off up the corridor. Once she had rounded the corner, she stood seething for a few moments. To think that she had let herself become attracted to him, and he was spinning her a web of lies! But of course, being a writer, he would be able to think up all sorts of stories! Maybe that tale of living with his Labrador in the countryside and the two older sisters was just a fabrication.

As she made her way back to her cabin, she surmised this was the problem with holiday romances. You had no proof of what the other person was telling you. By the time she got back, she was shaking with fury.

Aunt Ronnie was combing her hair at the mirror, and turned in surprise when Leda burst in.

'From the look on your face, something has got to you. What is it?'

218

Leda threw her bag on her bed and sat down, folding her arms. 'I can't believe it, Auntie! After my swim, I went to Nick's cabin because I had something to tell him — I'll explain in a minute — and I was a little cautious because I thought he might be with that young woman.'

'And was he?' Ronnie put her comb down.

'Yes, but that's not why I'm furious. They were having a meeting, would you believe?'

'What was strange about that?'

'Auntie, it turns out he's been lying to me all this time. Nick's not a freelance lawyer, he's actually a writer — and that young woman, Sophie, is his agent!'

Ronnie sat on her own bed. 'Well, at least they're not involved.'

'Auntie, that's not the point. What's so awful is that he's been spinning tales. For all I know he could live in London with a wife and three kids, and he's come on the cruise to escape and find some fun with other women!' Her mouth set mutinously.

Ronnie gave a great peal of laughter. 'Who's spinning stories now? Oh, Leda, I can't see Nick as the duplicitous lothario!' Then her face became more serious. 'Don't be so judgmental, dear. What else did he say?'

'He said they had to finish their meeting — I can't imagine what could be so urgent on a cruise! But he wants to meet me later so he can explain, he said. I said I'd meet him after dinner, at quarter to eight. But I'm not going to let him sweet-talk me. I knew it was a mistake, letting myself fall for him.' Her eyes filled with tears.

Ronnie came over and sat beside her, putting her arm around her shoulders. 'And have you fallen for him?' she said, gently.

'Oh, Auntie! I know I said I'd just have a flirtation, but he was so lovely with me, and I let myself be taken in. But it was all false!'

'Now, we don't know that at all,'

Ronnie chided, rubbing Leda's shoulder. 'Wait and see what he has to say for himself later. You may find it's not as black as it seems.'

* * *

They went for afternoon tea in the New York lounge, after which there was a quiz about crime novels. Leda tried to lose herself in the paperback she'd brought with her, while Ronnie took part in the quiz. They had an hour or so to fill until it was time to change for dinner — not that she felt like eating anything, but she tried to put her misgivings out of her mind, for Ronnie's sake. After all, the cruise was her great aunt's holiday, and though there was the tragedy of Tish Rundle's disappearance hanging over them, Leda felt that Ronnie deserved to enjoy herself.

Back in the cabin, she flicked through her wardrobe, and in the end, chose white trousers, with a flowery loose blouse in blues and reds. It was a cheerful outfit and she hoped it might lift her mood. Ronnie was wearing a midnight blue skirt with a pale blue top sprinkled with sparkly beads. Her white hair curled softly round her face and pink lipstick brought out the delicate colour of her perfect complexion. Leda thought what an attractive woman she was, even now, and that she must have been stunning when she was young. They smiled at each other in the mirror as they both made a final adjustment to their hair.

'Well, my dear, I don't know how any man could resist you!' Ronnie said. 'Now, remember to hold your head up high and believe in yourself, no matter what. Don't let this get you down. If it's a washout, just put it behind you and look to the future. Don't lose faith in love.'

Leda turned to her, putting her arms round her.

'Auntie, you're so good to me. You're right, I've been wallowing for too long since my relationship with Damien ended. And if Nick is going to let me down, I'll do my very best not to let it destroy my confidence. I know I'm a successful woman, and yes — I do feel attractive.'

'That's the way! Now, are we ready?'

As they entered the dining room, Leda mused, 'I wonder if Jason will come to dinner?' Their table was still set for four.

'I caught sight of him briefly earlier. I think one of the security team is keeping him company, making sure he's not left on his own. It must all be very traumatic for him, and they'll want to make sure he doesn't get too depressed.'

As it turned out, there was no sign of Jason during the time they were eating. They assumed he was either taking a meal in his room, or was somewhere with the security staff.

'Barcelona tomorrow.' Ronnie swirled her wine, looking into its golden depths. 'We have tickets on the bus tour — do you still want to go?'

'Yes, we must. It's the last day of your holiday, and after you missed Florence, you don't want to miss this. Do you feel up to it?' Leda asked.

'I'm fine now. My ankles have recovered completely. I looked at the weather forecast, and it seems it's going to be cloudy and much cooler, so I won't have any problems. We just have a couple of hours off the bus at lunchtime, so I won't be pounding the cobbles in the heat.'

They made their way to the Hollywood Lounge to look at what was on offer for the evening. Ronnie beamed when she saw the poster. 'Look, Hollywood legends — excerpts from *Singin' In The Rain*, *The Wizard of Oz*, *Some Like It Hot*, *Hello Dolly* and lots more. I shall enjoy that!'

Leda gave a little sigh of relief. If Aunt Ronnie was happy to watch the show, she could talk with Nick without worrying about her.

'Let's find a seat at the end of a row,

so I can slip out when I need to. Shall we meet up after?'

Ronnie patted her arm. 'Don't worry about me. I'll take myself up to the buffet for a cup of tea, and then off to bed. You can meet me there if you finish before ten, but if you're busy with Nick, don't break off just for me. You please yourself — it's your holiday too,' she added as Leda began to protest.

Leda gave in. 'I'll see how long we are.'

She glanced out of the window. Outside, the moon was just past full, shining on the water. It made her think of the lovely evening she and Nick had shared just a few nights earlier. What would tonight bring?

At that moment, one of the crew came over to her. 'Miss Leda Hollings? I have a message for you from the tour desk. They need to talk with you about your booking for the tour in Barcelona tomorrow. You must come now, as tour desk closes in half an hour.'

A wave of frustration made Leda

frown. 'But the show starts in ten minutes.'

'You can be back in time for the start, Miss. If you come quickly with me, I know short cut.'

Leda looked anxiously at Ronnie. 'Do you mind if you go in and find us a couple of seats? I'll be back as quickly as I can.'

Her aunt agreed, so Leda followed the man, who walked quickly as he cut down beside the lounge and through a door marked *Crew Only*. They walked along a narrow corridor lined with many doors, all closed.

As they reached the end of the corridor, Leda was aware of one of the doors opening behind her, but she thought nothing of it until an arm came round her from behind, pinning her arms to her side, and a hand clamped over her mouth.

Startled and afraid, she kicked back with her legs, but in one brisk movement, her assailant swung her round and thrust her into a tiny room.

She only had a brief glimpse of mops and buckets as she crashed to her knees, then the door swung shut behind her and she was plunged into darkness!

Immediately she scrambled to her feet and ran to the door, feeling for the handle. But there was an ominous click, and with horror and despair Leda realised she was locked in.

15

Leda pounded the door with her fists, but in the distance she was aware of the sound of the pre-show music starting in the Lounge. It would drown out her cries. Soon her eyes adjusted to the darkness, and she became aware that there was a tiny crack of light coming through the keyhole. Whoever had locked her in had obviously taken the key with them.

Eventually, her voice began to crack with shouting, and her arms and hands felt bruised with battering on the door, so she stopped. Turning her back to the door, she let herself slide to the floor, and rested her forehead on her knees. As the pounding of her heart began to lessen, she closed her eyes.

Why would anyone want to shut her in? It seemed incomprehensible.

From here Leda could hear nothing

except the faint dull thump of music through the walls, and had no idea whether anyone was passing in the corridor, or if it was all quiet.

Before long, wild scenarios began to pass through her mind . . . What if they didn't find her? How long would it take her to die of thirst? Her lively imagination pictured someone eventually opening the door to find her expired!

Then she gave a self-deprecating laugh and shook her head. She blinked away the self-pitying tears and made herself breathe deeply. She'd only been here a short time. She would survive overnight and Ronnie would raise the alarm if she was missing in the morning.

Feeling her way around the room, she realised it was full of cleaning gear — mops, buckets, brooms and vacuum cleaners — and a faint synthetic scent from some of the cleaning products. A crew member would probably come at some point to use them tomorrow morning. She didn't need to worry. And there must be a little air coming into the room, even if it was just through the keyhole.

While she sat there, she considered why anyone would want to lock her up. Had she been close to discovering something criminal? Was it to do with Tish's disappearance? Who was the crew member who had led her here? Was it significant that there was a woman on board who resembled Tish?

Eventually, the darkness as well as weariness caused by the aftermath of her distress made her doze a little. She wasn't sure how long she had been asleep when she heard the distinct sound of voices in the corridor. At last!

Leaping to her feet, she thumped on the door again, shouting, 'Help! Let me out! Help!'

To her relief, a voice on the other side responded, but she couldn't make out what they were saying.

Putting her mouth to the keyhole, she

called, 'I'm locked in! Please get me out!'

The voice replied, though she still couldn't hear the words. She could only assume they were sending for help, and forced herself to remain calm while that was coming.

After what seemed like an interminable time, there was the welcome rattle of a key in the lock, and the door swung open.

The sudden light was blinding, and Leda put her arm up to shield her eyes as she staggered into the corridor. She blnked furiously and saw a small Oriental female member of crew standing beside a tall figure in a white uniform — Iannis!

'Leda, how did you get in this room? Are you all right?' His voice was full of concern. For once there was no sign of the trademark white smile.

Her voice shaky, Leda replied, 'I don't know! A crew member was taking me to the excursion desk — he said there was a problem with the tickets for tomorrow's tour. He told me this was a short cut, but someone caught me and threw me into this cupboard.'

'Did you see the person who did this?'

She shook her head. 'No, he came from behind. It must have been a man — he was tall and strong.'

Iannis thanked the Oriental woman and said she could go now and he would deal with the matter. Then he turned back to Leda.

'Are you all right? I will take you to your great aunt, as she is waiting at the Reception Desk. She has been very worried about you. Can you walk?'

Leda realised she was in fact quite all right, though a bit disorientated by the light. She straightened her back and looked him in the eyes. 'I'm fine. What time is it?'

'Almost ten o'clock.'

The second performance of the show must have been nearing its conclusion, as she could hear music and applause from the Lounge.

'We'll go this way.' He took her along to the end of the corridor, where they looped round and emerged from a door on the other side of the ship. They had to climb up a deck to reach the Reception Desk.

As they reached the Reception area, there were a few people asking questions at the desk, as was usual on the cruise. But Leda only had eyes for the small figure sitting in one of the comfortable seats, her hands resting on her walking stick.

'Aunt Ronnie!' She rushed over to her side.

Her aunt looked up and exclaimed with feeling. 'Leda! Oh, thank God! I was so worried when you didn't reappear. What happened? Are you all right, dear?' She struggled to her feet, suddenly looking every one of her eighty-three years.

Leda enveloped her in a hug.

'I was shut in a cupboard! But I'm fine. How are you? I'm so sorry you had this worry!'

It was only then she became aware that there was someone else sitting near Ronnie — Nick. Her heart thumped, seeing him and the concern in his expression. She directed a weary smile at him. Then she felt a hand on her shoulder, and looked round to find Iannis, his face serious.

'Would you like something to drink? Water, or something stronger?' he asked.

Aware that her throat was parched, she nodded. 'Thank you — water would be fine.'

'I have informed the security officer of this incident. She would like to see you in her office.'

Ronnie grasped her arm. 'I'm coming with you. I want to hear what happened.'

Nick also accompanied them, so all three of them crowded into the office of Marika, the chief Security Officer.

Iannis returned with a bottle of spring water and then left again before they started the discussion. Leda moistened her throat with it before she began to tell the story of her imprisonment. Marika listened intently throughout the account.

After hearing that Leda hadn't seen the man who threw her into the supply cupboard, she asked, 'Could you describe this member of crew who escorted you down the corridor? Did he have a name badge?' Every member of crew, except the captain, wore a badge stating their name and position on the ship.

Leda realised Marika had a slight accent, and wondered briefly at her country of origin, before giving her reply. 'No, I don't remember seeing a badge. He was wearing a red jacket, and looked to be Asian, possibly Filipino, but a description . . . all I can say is that he came up to my shoulder, and was slim in build, no distinguishing marks.'

Marika nodded. A large proportion of the crew were from that part of the world, and the description Leda had given would cover most of the male Filipino crew.

'Would you recognise him again?'

Leda thought for a moment, then sighed. 'I doubt it. I didn't take much notice of him. I'm sorry.' She felt Nick's hand on hers and looked up to see sympathy in his eyes.

The Security Officer laid down her pen. 'Well, I shall make further enquiries, and hope to discover what this was all about. I'm so sorry this should happen on board our ship. Please let me know if you remember anything else.'

When they emerged, Leda was distracted for a moment by photographs of the senior crew displayed for the benefit of passengers. Marika's was especially good. The Security Officer's country of origin was Lithuania, which accounted for the attractive accented English.

She pushed it from her mind as Ronnie smiled at her wearily. 'All I can say is I'm so thankful you're safe, my dear. After what happened to Tish Rundle, you can imagine my thoughts!'

Leda hugged her. 'I'm devastated that you should have this worry. Would you like to go for a cup of tea now?'

Ronnie gave a small laugh. 'I've had enough tea to launch a ship! I think I'll just go to bed.'

Leda and Nick walked Ronnie back to the cabin. As they neared the door, Nick asked, 'What about you, Leda? You must be exhausted after your ordeal.'

Ronnie opened the door with her card and turned to look at them.

'Why not go and spend some time together? It will do you good, rather than going to bed with that nasty experience uppermost in your mind. I won't worry about you knowing you're with Nick.'

'Your aunt's right, Leda. Please, come. I'd still like to explain things, as I said earlier.'

'All right. If you're really sure you don't mind being alone, Auntie.'

Ronnie shooed them off. 'I think I'll go straight to sleep. As long as Nick doesn't let you out of his sight, I'm quite happy.'

Nick suggested Leda should wear something warmer, and waited outside the cabin while she changed into jeans and a jumper, and grabbed her jacket.

They made their way back up the stairs.

'Where are we going?' Leda asked. Now she was alone with him, she could feel the pull of his charisma again, and steeled herself to be strong. Although she wanted to trust him, she didn't know if she would be wise to do so.

'I want to show you something.'

He turned and smiled at her, and she felt that familiar treacherous flip in her chest.

Suddenly something crossed her mind.

'Where's Sophie? Not with you tonight?'

'Sophie has plenty of her own things to do. She went to see the show, and she's probably in one of the bars now. She's only here for a couple of days, as she's giving a talk tomorrow and will be be bombarded by many hopeful writers. I insisted she make the most of her free time.'

'But not with you . . .'

He shook his head wearily. 'I told you, Sophie's an agent. She's a junior in the firm, but my own agent is grooming her and lets her take on some of my business. She's a 'touchy feely' type, you might say, and very effusive, which is probably why you were confused. But she has a boyfriend back home. I'm one of her charges, and she's determined to look after me. I'm equally determined she's not to keep me on a leash.'

Leda didn't know quite how to respond, as she was still feeling prickly about the whole secret identity business. Maybe she would change her opinion once she knew what he was going to explain to her.

They reached the deck where the

information about the crime writing events was laid out. No one was looking at it at this time of night. Walking towards the exhibition, he stood in front of the panels and faced her.

'Notice anything?'

Leda frowned, casting her gaze over the posters and photos, then back to his face.

'Not really,' she said.

He pointed to the photo of Harry Agnew.

'See any resemblance?' He fished in his pocket and brought out his glasses, putting them on. 'What about now?'

Studying the picture carefully, then glancing back at his face, she gasped as recognition clicked. 'You're Harry Agnew! What happened to the beard?'

He gave a sheepish grin. 'I had it a couple of years, and somehow it became my official photo. But I felt it was time for a change — and it helped me have a holiday incognito without lots of fans interrupting me.'

A couple approached and began

leafing through the information, glancing towards Nick and Leda. He quickly turned away and took off his glasses, so no one else would make the connection.

'Leda, there's a lot I'd like to say to you, but this isn't the place. Let's go out on deck.'

16

Looking into Nick's eyes, Leda believed she could see honesty in his gaze, so she agreed. There were too many people around these indoor areas to talk seriously without interruptions. It was cool out on deck at this hour, which would put off most of the passengers.

It took Leda a few moments to realise he had brought her to the Promenade Deck, the very place they had spent that romantic evening. He even managed to find the same table.

Further along the deck there were two other couples sitting with drinks, but she suspected they wouldn't stay long, as they were still dressed in their light clothes for dinner, and the wind was chilly now that the ship was sailing.

Nick took Leda's hand and pulled her into one seat, then sat opposite her.

'There's some shelter here, but let

me know when you want to go back inside.'

'Nick, there's something I haven't mentioned . . . ' Leda took a deep breath, then pushed on before she lost her nerve. 'When I saw you in Rome, I overheard your conversation on your phone on the steps of St Peter's. You were saying you were relieved no one had recognised you, or worked out who you really were.'

To her surprise, Nick burst out laughing. 'I suppose you thought I was a criminal on the run?'

'I didn't know what to think! Surely it's not so bad, being a famous writer? Why all the secrecy?'

The mirth went from his face, replaced by seriousness.

'I don't mind being recognised, and of course it's good for book sales when people meet the author. I haven't done any public appearances for over a year, because I had a very bad experience . . . It must be a couple of years ago now that one of my fans became obsessed with me.

'It started off with the usual fan letter, saying how much she enjoyed my books. But then she began sending cards for my birthday, for Valentine's Day and Christmas — and they came to my home address, not to my agent. She had managed to find out where I was living in London.

'Then the deliveries started — flowers, chocolates, fruit. After a while it became clear she was bringing these in person. The letters continued, and her writing became angry, accusing me of ignoring her. The diatribes began to take the tone of an aggrieved lover, and she started making references to meetings that had never happened. I don't know whether she really believed they had taken place, or whether it was just a ploy to get my attention . . .

'Finally I came home one evening to find her waiting for me. She threw herself into my arms on my doorstep. I took her into my flat — big mistake, but I didn't want her disturbing my neighbours. She became hysterical, accusing me of deserting her and being callous. To my horror, she actually pulled a knife and tried to stab me!

'I was able to restrain her and take it off her, but it was a huge shock. She collapsed, weeping, and at that point I called the police. Thankfully they believed me, as she was clearly in a state of mental trauma. She wasn't charged in the end, for which I'm glad, because she was mentally ill. I heard later that she was receiving treatment.

'But it shook me, and I realised I was more vulnerable than I imagined. I changed agents, as I thought I hadn't been protected sufficiently, and decided to move into the country.'

His face took on a more peaceful demeanour.

'It was one of the best things I've ever done. I found the cottage in Derbyshire, and acquired my dog, who has been the best companion.'

'Did you have a girlfriend at the time?'

'I had been seeing someone, but she couldn't stand the countryside. She was a real city girl. Once I'd moved, I realised I had found my true home. I was at peace.'

He looked up, and took her hand.

'Yes, I'm lonely at times, and I do believe having someone special to share it with is better than just me and the dog. But it has to be the right person.'

Leda felt the pressure of his fingers, and she looked at their intertwined hands lit by the solitary tea-light flickering in a glass on the table.

'So you don't make many forays into civilisation these days?'

He sighed. 'I must confess that, apart from the odd visit to London to my agent, I've only visited family in the past year. It was a bit of an adventure, coming on the cruise. My current agent pressed me to take the speaking engagement because it would be good for book sales and said it was time I emerged from hibernation. When she told me the cruise company would throw in a free cruise for the week as part of my payment, I thought, *why not?* It's ages since I had a holiday, and I can be in company with people without having to join in if I didn't want to. But then I met you, and I realised what I'd been missing . . . '

Leda withdrew her hand, uncertain what to think. Had she just been a first taste of romance for him after a long gap without anyone in his life? Or did this really mean something?

'Have I said something to upset you?'

She turned to look at him.

'It's just been rather strange for me, too. I came on this holiday at the last minute to look after Aunt Ronnie, and somehow I've ended up meeting you, which I didn't expect.

'I was convinced I didn't want anything to do with men, after what happened with Damien, my last boyfriend. He was controlling and constantly undermining my confidence. It took a long time to acknowledge to myself that I wasn't

247

guilty of all the faults he said I had. I broke it off about a year ago, but we'd been together for nearly two years.

'It was Aunt Ronnie who convinced me I was ready to open myself up to a 'fling' as she put it.'

She was trying to keep her voice light. She didn't want Nick to know she had fallen for him as hard. By pushing it to the back of her mind, she was certain she could convince herself that she'd only had a little bit of fun on the cruise, that her heart wasn't in danger.

'Is that what this is? A fling?'

He reached out for her hand again, looking deeply into her eyes. The earnestness of his gaze made her resolve falter. How she longed to abandon herself to his attention.

'I . . . I don't know . . . Is it?'

'All I know is that I want to keep doing this . . .'

He leaned forward and pressed his lips to hers, then his arms came round her again. With a sigh, she moulded herself to him, feeling the deep pulsing of desire through her body.

At length they pulled away.

Without saying any more, Nick pulled his chair round until they were sitting elbow to elbow and he could put his arm round her. He kissed her hair, and she laid her head on his shoulder.

Don't think of the future, she told herself. *Just enjoy the now.*

They sat in silence for some time, aware of the sounds around them — the sea rushing against the sides of the ship as it ploughed through the Mediterranean, the flapping of a flag in the breeze, the distant hum of music and voices from inside the ship as doors opened and closed. Occasionally someone walked by, but the other couple had long gone from their table.

Eventually, Nick spoke again, in a low voice.

'After my stalker had been stopped and my existence returned to normal, I looked at my sisters and their family lives and realised I'd had enough of the high life. I'm much happier living in

Derbyshire now. I believe when you're content, you're more open to love. What do you think?'

Leda thought for a while. 'I am content, that's what Aunt Ronnie made me see. I've been able to put my hurt behind me now, and enjoy my success in my career and with my friends.'

'And are you open to love?'

He put a finger under her chin and turned her face so that their lips were nearly touching.

'I . . . I think so . . . '

Again they kissed, and Leda let the intense sensations pour over her.

When they parted and once more she was in the curve of his arm, he said, 'Tell me about yourself, right from the start. I want to know everything.'

With a laugh, she said, 'It's not very interesting.'

'It is to me.'

She gave in, and they exchanged more of the details of their lives. The hours went by without them realising, until Leda gave a huge yawn.

'You need some sleep, you've had quite a day. And Ronnie said you're taking a trip tomorrow.'

'I suppose so. I do want to visit Barcelona, and if we don't, it'll be a disappointment for us both.'

They spoke in low voices, barely audible. The candle had long ago guttered and gone out. Then Nick gripped her arm. Alarmed, she looked at him, and he held a finger to his lips, pointing to the deck below. The tang of cigarette smoke drifted up in the wind.

There were two figures in the area allotted to the crew for recreation. It was almost three o'clock, and everyone, even the hardiest of revellers, had gone to bed. But there were two distinct shapes against the rail — a man and a woman. Leda and Nick couldn't hear what they were saying, but they were clearly arguing. As Leda watched, she realised the man was Jason Rundle, and the woman could have been Tish! Or was it her lookalike?

They gesticulated angrily at each other, the woman eventually turning away, taking a strong drag on her cigarette. The illumination from the deck lights confirmed that it was indeed the woman Leda had mistaken for Tish. Jason gripped her shoulder, but she threw his hand off, turning to wave her finger menacingly at him.

Eventually she stalked off, towards the interior of the ship, with Jason following her closely.

When Nick was sure they had gone, he nodded to Leda, and spoke in a low voice. 'Well — that was certainly Jason Rundle. Was that his wife?'

'No, that's the woman I told you about, the one I thought was Tish. The resemblance is amazing.'

'So, could she be a sister? She must be a member of the crew — though how the likeness escaped them, I don't know.'

'It's easy to make yourself look different. If she wore a lot of make-up, and arranged her hair differently, people wouldn't make the connection.'

Nick put his chin on his hand, thinking.

'Well, still no sign of Tish, but this woman must be involved.'

'Not necessarily. It could just be they were talking about Tish, and still don't know where or how she disappeared.'

'I don't think so, Leda. Why would they meet at the dead of night, where they thought no one would see them? They were very careful to keep to that part of the deck — maybe it's an area that isn't covered by security cameras. If there was nothing sinister going on, they would meet openly. I think we should inform the security team about what we've seen.'

Leda contemplated this for a moment, then agreed. With Nick's law training and his author's creativeness, his mind was more alert when it came to looking out for criminal motives and intent.

'All right. I always thought the

Rundles were strange — Jason in particular. If there's something unlawful going on here, we need to expose it. And Tish is still missing and she may be in danger. There's nothing to be lost. Should we do it first thing in the morning?'

'No, we're doing it now. Every hour, every minute could count in this investigation. We reach Barcelona early tomorrow, and if we leave it until after we dock, we could be too late.'

The decks were subdued, and when they reached the information desk, there was no one in sight.

Nick was just about to walk behind the counter to knock at the office door, when a crew member came out. Fair and tanned, he wore a white uniform like all the senior officers. He stopped at the sight of the two of them standing at the desk.

'May I help you? Is something wrong?' His accent sounded Australian.

'Is Marika still on duty? We'd like to tell her something we think could be connected with Tish Rundle's disappearance.'

'I'm afraid she's off duty now. She'll be here in the morning at nine o'clock.' At their disconcerted expression, he added, 'Can I help you? I'm Freddy, assistant security officer. I've been involved in this investigation, so I'm fully up to speed with it. What do you have to tell me?'

'We're acquaintances of Jason Rundle, and Leda here was one of the couple's dinner companions. We're fully aware of all that's going on with the investigation into Tish Rundle's disappearance. We've been up on deck since about half past ten, and believe we've seen something that may be connected with the case.'

Freddy nodded. 'Right, come with me into the security office.'

They followed him in and at his invitation sat in the two chairs in front of the desk.

'If you could explain everything . . . ' He pulled out a drawer and retrieved a large folder, opening it on the desk and reaching for a pen.

'All right if I begin the talking?' Nick asked Leda, and she agreed. He gave the officer their names, and a brief outline of their backgrounds, before telling him what they had seen from their vantage point on deck.

'I believe I've seen this woman before — twice,' Leda continued after Nick had finished his explanation. 'Before Tish disappeared, I was passing the Rundles' cabin, and thought I saw two women emerging, but before I could register it, someone knocked me over. It was Jason who picked me up, and there was no sign of a second woman at this point. But now I think he knocked me down himself, pretending someone else had done it, to hide the fact that there was a woman who looked very like Tish on board.'

Freddy looked at her searchingly.

'But you can't be sure.'

Her heart sinking, Leda replied, 'No, but I did speak to this woman yesterday

— I saw her on deck, and thought it was Tish. But when I caught up with her, I saw it was just a very strong resemblance. She *does* exist.'

'I'm not disputing that. There does seem to be something going on. One of our staff left Mr Rundle at his cabin at ten o'clock. He said he was exhausted and wanted to sleep. But it looks like he has another agenda. Mr Drake, Miss Hollings, you can leave this in our hands. I'll contact the head of the British team immediately.'

Leda and Nick left the office. She felt a shiver run through her, and Nick put his arm round her.

'Go to bed, you're tired.'

'How will we know what happens? Auntie and I will be on a bus tomorrow . . . I mean, later today.'

'Here, put your number in my phone, and I'll do the same for you. Sophie is giving a workshop in the morning, after which we're going over my talk for the evening. I'll keep in touch and let you know what's going on.'

When they reached Leda's cabin Nick encircled her in his arms, his cheek on her hair. Then he gave her a lingering kiss, making her heart somersault. They wished each other goodnight, parting reluctantly.

Leda crept into the darkened cabin, glad of the moonlight seeping through the porthole to give her some illumination as she prepared for bed. Soon she slipped beneath the bedcovers, and though her mind and emotions were whirling, she quickly dropped into a deep sleep.

17

Leda opened her heavy eyes to find Ronnie standing over her, fully dressed. She groaned and rolled over.

'Wake up, sleepy head! We're in Barcelona.'

'I'm so late! No time for a run this morning.'

'You'll need to be quick with your shower if we're to get breakfast before we go on the trip. You must have had a late night last night.'

Her aunt's eyes twinkled. Leda sat up, and stretched. 'Yes, we were late.'

'I hope you weren't going over your nasty experience earlier.'

Surprisingly, Leda had forgotten about being locked in. She wondered whether to tell her aunt, but in the end there was no time, just a rush to get ready, and then in the breakfast room there was no privacy. But it would have to come out at some point.

The weather was slightly overcast, though the air felt pleasantly warm. They joined their bus with a few minutes to spare, and sat back to be taken round the sights.

Leda had spent a weekend in the city a few years earlier, but it was the first time for Ronnie. Their guide pointed out the most famous sights, and they had the chance to disembark for a short time at the cathedral of the Sagrada Familia, designed by the architect Antoni Gaudi and started in 1882.

Ronnie was amazed that it was still under construction after so many years. She bought a guide book to read later. 'Has much changed since you were here?' she asked Leda.

'Yes, it looks very different,' she replied over the noise of the construction. The guide pointed out the newest parts, but they didn't have time to queue to go inside. Instead they were taken around the cathedral, and to view a model of how it would look when completed.

'You must come back and see it when it's finished,' Ronnie said as she gazed at the model.

Leda leaned in to examine the model.

'I'll bring you as well,' she said with a smile.

Ronnie laughed. 'It would be nice to think I would last that long! Still . . . ' she took Leda's arm as they made their way out of the shop, 'I've had such fun seeing all these new places that I'm definitely considering another cruise next year.'

'Good! I'm glad you've enjoyed yourself, despite everything.'

They strolled back to the bus.

'It's been far more exciting than I ever imagined. Not only am I visiting lots of places I've only read about — not to mention seeing the Pope in person! — but there's been a real life mystery on board! *And* I've seen a new romance evolving to boot.' She gave

Leda a mischievous look.

Leda blushed. 'I don't know if it's going to come to anything, but our time together last night was special. I felt that Nick was beginning to open up to me, and I could relax in his company. But you know, Auntie, it's a difficult situation. We don't live anywhere near each other. What will happen when the cruise is over?'

'Well, that's for you two to work out.'

They stood near the bus, and as there was no one nearby, Leda decided to reveal to Ronnie more of her news.

'There's something I haven't told you about Nick. You'll be going to the talk by Harry Agnew tonight, won't you?'

'Just try to keep me away! I'll be in the front of the queue to get my book signed as well!'

'You don't need to queue, Auntie. You've been in his company for the last few days.'

Ronnie frowned. 'You don't mean to say . . . that Nick is actually Harry Agnew?'

Giggling at her astonished expression, Leda nodded. 'Harry was his father's name, and Agnew was his grandmother's maiden name. He shaved off his beard a few months ago, and decided to take a holiday incognito.'

'Well, fancy that! He's a dark horse.' Ronnie suddenly looked worried. 'I hope I didn't say anything foolish when we were talking about crime novels the other day.'

'I'm sure you didn't. But there's something else . . . ' She went on to tell her great aunt about the sighting of Jason Rundle with the lookalike woman on the crew deck, and their visit to the security officer.

'That does sound very suspicious. You did the right thing, going to the security people. I take it you haven't heard anything more from Nick.'

They climbed on the bus. 'Nothing — maybe it was all quite innocent.'

The tour continued round the city, finally stopping near La Rambla in Barcelona's main shopping centre, where they were given two hours for lunch and sightseeing.

After having a snack, the two women wandered down the long, broad street, looking at the stalls in the centre, and the aviaries attached to the pet shop stalls. They sat for a while on a bench, just watching the bustle of the tourist crowds enjoying the vibrant atmosphere. Ronnie commented that she had never seen so many nationalities in one place — people carrying shopping bags from fashionable shops, others snapping pictures on mobile phones, some in shorts, others dressed smartly. A babble of different languages reached them in bursts as they watched the people go by.

★ ★ ★

They returned to meet their bus at the rendezvous point just before two o'clock. Leda felt her eyes closing as they were taken round a final circuit of the city, her late night catching up with her. When she blinked and stirred, she was surprised to find they could already see the ship.

She looked at her watch as the bus drew up on the quayside.

'It's barely half past three. I thought we weren't going to return until four thirty. There are no other buses back yet.'

'Maybe the bus driver's ready for a siesta — I know I am!' Ronnie yawned as they gathered their bags and jackets. 'Although I could do with a cup of tea first.'

'I'll text Nick to tell him we're back early.'

It only took her a few moments, but they were the last people to leave the bus. Leda helped Aunt Ronnie down from the bus, thanking the driver and the guide at the door as they passed. The other bus passengers had stepped out ahead of them and had already boarded the ship, but Leda strolled slowly to accommodate Ronnie's pace.

At the foot of the gangplank, Ronnie halted.

'Just a moment, Leda. I thought my boarding pass was in my pocket. I must have put it in my handbag. Let me search for it before we go on board. I don't want to hold anyone up at security.'

Ronnie's bag was capacious, with many little pockets, so it took them some time before the missing card came to light. Leda heaved a sigh of relief. This was the last time they would use their cards, save for disembarking when they went to the airport tomorrow. It wouldn't do to lose Ronnie's at this late hour.

As everyone else had boarded the ship long ahead of them, no one else was on the gangplank as they made their way up. When they reached the top and plunged into the gloom of the ship's interior, Leda felt in her small shoulder bag for her own pass. When she looked up to hand it over, she was astonished to be looking at Iannis.

He looked equally surprised and frowned at her appearance. 'Leda! I thought you were out on a bus tour.'

'We have been — we seem to have arrived back early. We're the tail end of the group, as Auntie can't walk quickly.'

Ronnie had gone ahead, checked through by the other attendant. Leda's eyes had accustomed to the lower light inside, and when she looked at the person on duty with Iannis, she gave a gasp of recognition. This was the crew member who had lured her down the corridor last night!

'Iannis, this is the crewman who gave me the false message before I was locked in!'

Looking at the officer, his face was stern. He said nothing. Puzzled by his lack of reaction, she began to repeat her accusation.

Then she heard her aunt exclaim, 'Tish! You're safe! How wonderful!'

Beyond the security checkpoint, Ronnie was standing in front of a woman who was indeed Tish Rundle.

At that moment, Nick appeared from the stairs, and took in the scene with a glance. He grabbed Tish's arm. Leda was flung aside as Iannis dived through the security arch towards the pair, and swung a punch at Nick. Luckily he saw it coming and ducked, so the officer's fist swept harmlessly past his face.

As the two men began to wrestle, Tish launched herself towards the security point. She held out a card to the small crewman who scanned it quickly. Instinctively Leda stepped in front of her, barring her way.

'Oh, no you don't! You're not getting away this time. You've disrupted this cruise enough!'

She grasped Tish by her upper arms. No matter how much the other woman struggled, she wasn't as tall or as fit as Leda, and she couldn't break free. Leda gritted her teeth and kept hold of her, even when Tish attempted to kick her shins.

Beyond the checkpoint, Ronnie shouted loudly for security.

A security officer must have been on the floor above, as he came to help Nick with Iannis. Another followed soon after. Within moments, Tish, Iannis, and their crewman friend were pinned by the arms, and escorted back upstairs.

'Auntie — are you all right?' Leda gasped.

'I'm fine — all I did was call for help. You two were so brave! To think we've solved the mystery — at least, I think we have! I hope we find out what it was all about.'

Nick grinned, pushing his hair from his eyes.

'You did your part, too — I don't know if I would have succeeded in subduing that officer if your cries for help hadn't summoned security.'

Leda suggested they drop their bags off in their cabin and then all meet for tea in the lounge. 'Although Auntie may want a rest after all that excitement.'

'I've woken up now! All that action certainly got the juices flowing,' Ronnie laughed.

* * *

Twenty minutes later they were sitting in the afternoon tea lounge, surrounded by other passengers who were sipping tea and eating dainty cakes, oblivious of the drama that had taken place so recently on the gangway.

Nick was demolishing a large buttered scone topped with jam.

'We have to go to the security office in an hour. I dropped in at Marika's on my way up here, and she said she wanted to speak to us. I expect the Spanish police will have a few questions, too.'

In between replenishing their energy with tea and cakes, they spent their time speculating about what had been going on, but without answers they could only guess.

At quarter to five they arrived at Marika's office, where they were ushered inside immediately. The Chief Security Officer, looking smart and efficient as usual, introduced them to an English-speaking policeman from the Barcelona force, who shook their hands.

He took statements from all of them, which didn't take long, then he politely took his leave.

'I don't suppose you can tell us the whole story?' Ronnie asked as soon as he'd left.

Marika closed the folder on the desk in front of her and looked at the elderly lady over the top of her glasses. Then the corners of her lips twitched.

'I can see that you're not going to be satisfied with anything less than the complete truth.'

18

Nick grinned. 'Presumably the whole setup was to fake Tish Rundle's death? And I assume that the lookalike woman from the entertainment group had something to do with it, as well as the Greek officer?'

Marika nodded, and pushed the folder to one side. 'This was all part of an insurance scam. Jason and Letitia Rundle had taken out large life insurance policies, and the idea was that the wife's disappearance would result eventually in a huge payout.'

'Just a minute,' Leda interrupted. 'Did you say Letitia? That means that the note I found in our cabin on the first day was probably intended for Tish. It was addressed with a letter L.'

'But we're not even on the same deck,' Ronnie pointed out.

'No, but their cabin is directly above

ours. Whoever delivered it must have mistaken the deck number.'

'That's possible,' Marika admitted. 'Anyway, Letitia Rundle's sister, Chloe, has been a dancer with the entertainment troupe since the winter season. Chloe gave them the idea that lots of people go missing from cruise ships each year.'

'Is that right? I thought cruises were very safe.' Ronnie looked worried.

'Yes, they are — the casualties tend to be people who are fooling around on deck, ignoring the safety rules, usually drunk. For everyone else, it's very safe. Naturally we don't publicise this.

'Jason planned it very carefully. They chose this cruise because the last port of call was in Spain, and the couple had a property on the Costa Brava in Chloe's name. Tish would live there, pretending to be her sister. Once Tish had been officially declared dead, Jason would receive a substantial insurance payment. The two of them were going to meet up somewhere across the other side of the world, and live a life of luxury. Of course, her sister was to get money, plus the property in Spain.'

'What a devious scheme — and all for money.' Leda was astonished.

'Somehow, I think Jason enjoyed working it all out,' Nick commented.

'Yes,' Ronnie added. 'That young man certainly fancied himself as a clever clogs. I'm sure he would get a kick out of outwitting the authorities. To think I was sorry for him!'

'He was certainly a good actor. So where does Iannis come into all of this — and why was I shut in a store cupboard?' Leda queried.

'Iannis is Chloe's boyfriend. I admit I was surprised to see him flirting with you, as I had seen them together. I thought perhaps they had fallen out, but I believe he was trying to keep an eye on you and make sure you didn't discover the Rundles' plan. Presumably they thought you might question the resemblance between Chloe and Mrs Rundle if you saw her. Iannis had a member of the crew in his pay, who led you into the corridor where there were store cupboards. They didn't mean to hurt you, I believe.'

'I suppose they thought I might begin to make a connection between the sisters if I was watching Chloe for the duration of a whole show. They had tried to put us off going to an earlier show before.'

'And remember that the Rundles moved dining tables when they discovered Jackie and Steve both had a background in law?' Ronnie added. 'They must have wanted to avoid getting too close to them in case they sussed what was going on.'

'I suppose they thought an elderly lady and a young woman would be a softer option. Although it must have been a coincidence that I received the note and thought it was for me.'

Leda looked at Ronnie, who nodded.

'They would have been better off just going to the cafeteria to eat,' Nick put in.

'Ah, but they told us they really enjoyed the cruise experience — that must have been their downfall,' Ronnie pointed out. 'They should have kept a low profile instead of taking part in everything.'

'Plus it was a mistake to choose a crime writing cruise, with all these amateur sleuths and aspiring crime writers!' Leda giggled.

'So where is Jason?' Nick asked. 'Has he been apprehended?'

'Yes, he was still in the cabin,' Marika replied. 'The two British investigators are with him. He was going to complete the cruise as if his wife had really disappeared. But Tish was all too willing to tell us the truth when we caught her. She collapsed and confessed everything to the police, here in my office. I believe her husband was the brains behind the plan.'

Once they left Marika's office, they strolled back towards Leda and Ronnie's cabin, mulling over what they had heard.

'I wonder why Jason quarrelled with her sister that night we saw them on deck,' Leda said.

'Who knows? Maybe Chloe was getting cold feet.' Nick stood back so the two women could proceed down the corridor to their cabin.

'Or she wanted more money,' Ronnie added.

Leda turned to her in mock horror. 'Auntie, you're getting too immersed in this crime business. I think it's time we went home.'

But as she said this, her heart sank, knowing that soon she would be parted from Nick. Who knew what would happen now?

Ronnie gave a sigh. 'I can't believe our holiday is nearly over. But I'm looking forward to tonight.' She shook a finger at Nick. 'To think you deceived me all this time, and when I was wittering on about Harry Agnew's books, you never let on that you had written them!'

He smiled at her kindly. 'I know, I felt

really guilty about that. But I didn't know if you would spread the gossip if I told you the truth.' At the flash of her eyes, he added, 'I know, I know, you're probably one of the best people at keeping a secret. But I didn't know you well enough then. I would trust you with my life, now.'

Ronnie tapped him on the arm. 'There's no need for that, but as long as you promise me a prime seat for your talk, and to sign my book, I'll count that as recompense.'

He glanced at his watch, then looked at Leda apologetically. 'I'm going to have to leave you, grab a bite to eat, and then get ready for my talk.'

Leda put out a hand to stop him. 'I don't know what you planned, but there are two spare places at our dining table, and first sitting starts in half an hour. Would you and Sophie like to join us?'

'Oh, please do!' Ronnie's eyes sparkled.

He only had to consider for a moment. 'That sounds like a great idea.

I'm sure Sophie will be pleased to meet you both.'

★   ★   ★

An hour later, Sophie drew many admiring glances when Nick brought her to the table. She was wearing a bright red dress that hugged her perfect figure and showed off her long legs, enhanced by towering heels in the same hue. Her blonde hair was pinned up with a red flower.

Leda had to admit she looked stunning, and wondered how Nick could resist her. Then she stopped herself. He had said Sophie had a boyfriend back home. And all those kisses and caresses from him had felt genuine. She had to get over this lack of confidence! She decided to believe his words and enjoy the evening.

Sophie put her hand on Ronnie's arm as soon as they had sat down. 'You just have to tell me everything about your exciting time this afternoon! Nick refused to explain it all, just that you all had a part in resolving the mystery of the disappearing passenger. He said that it would be better if you all told me your own parts in it.'

She lifted her glass of red wine and took a large swig, her eyes sparkling.

As they explained how the mystery had unfolded, Sophie listened eagerly, exclaiming and encouraging them at each new revelation.

'And you really had no idea Jason was faking?'

'He did seem genuinely distressed when he showed us the security camera footage,' Ronnie replied, her expression grim. The others gave murmurs of agreement.

Eventually the talk moved on to other matters. Sophie turned out to be very good company, entertaining them with stories about her clients — without naming any names!

But for Leda it was the nearness of Nick, enjoying a social occasion with him in a normal way, that made it the best evening of the cruise. The conversation flowed, and they laughed frequently. To think she had thought it would be boring, coming on a cruise with an old lady! Ronnie was so lovely, so full of life. Of course, it wasn't usual to be part of a mystery on a holiday, either! At least no one had been hurt, which was the most important factor.

The wine was almost finished when Nick sighed. 'I'm sorry to break up this entertaining party, but time is getting on, and I need to prepare for my talk. I'm expected in the Hollywood Lounge for a sound check, then I want to check my notes.'

'I'll stay, if that's all right. You don't need me, do you, Nick?' Sophie drained her glass.

'No — I'll see you all later.'

His eyes flashed a special look at Leda, which made her heart flutter. Her feelings were veering between elation and despair, knowing they would be parting tomorrow, and wondering how he would leave matters between them.

Could this really be any more than a holiday romance?

The three women stayed for another fifteen minutes. As Leda stood, she noticed something glinting on the floor.

'Look, isn't that Nick's phone? it must have dropped out of his pocket.'

Sophie held out her hand. 'I'll see him before the talk, so if you give it to me I'll pass it on.'

Leda handed it over without another thought.

★   ★   ★

Later as she sat with Ronnie in the Hollywood Lounge, it gave her a thrill to see him as an author with a theatre full of adoring fans. Little did they know that those lips that were speaking had kissed her passionately and that commanding voice had whispered loving words into her ear!

It would have been nice just to relax like Aunt Ronnie and enjoy an entertaining talk by an author, but her mind ran through all their encounters since that first time when he had teased her in the cold pool. Every nerve remembered his strong body against hers when they were in the church in Florence, his lips exploring her own so enticingly.

Finally, Nick read an extract from his newest book, to be published the next month.

Leda wrenched her mind back to the present, and let herself be gripped by the plot. His voice was deep and expressive, and the story exciting. It left everyone on the edge of their seats — no doubt itching to purchase the book as soon as it was available.

Nick's talk came to a close, and applause filled the packed lounge. Instantly a queue formed to have books signed. Sophie appeared on stage beside him, to help deal with fans so they approached one by one and didn't crowd him.

'I can see he's going to be some time. Let's go and have a cup of tea.' Ronnie stood up.

With a sigh, Leda agreed, and
followed her out.

284

19

After about half an hour, Leda slipped back down to the lounge to see if Nick was almost finished. The queue still snaked round the aisles. He was chatting animatedly with an elderly man who had handed him a book. As she watched, Nick finished signing it and gave it back with a smile. The next woman stepped up quickly, her face shiny with excitement.

Leda returned to the coffee bar.

'He's going to be ages.' Her voice was flat, her shoulders slumped. 'You know, we ought to go and do our packing. The instructions we received earlier told us we have to put our sealed cases outside the cabin door by midnight, so they can be scanned and placed on the quayside for us to collect tomorrow morning.'

Ronnie agreed that it would be a good idea.

'What time is our flight?'

'One o'clock — but we have to leave at ten in the morning.'

Not much time to see Nick, she thought. She had hoped they would be able to spend another romantic evening together. But she would have to pack everything she didn't want to go in her hand luggage, so she would have to put on her travelling clothes tonight. A change of underwear and overnight things was all she could leave out. A gloomy cloud settled on her at the thought of leaving the Ocean Star and all it had held for her.

They emptied the wardrobes and drawers, and soon had their cases packed. At that point, there was a knock on the cabin door.

Leda's heart leaped.

When she opened the door, it wasn't Nick, but a woman in crew uniform.

'I'm so glad I found you,' she said. 'There's been a last minute change to your flight. Technical problems. The flight to Newcastle was cancelled. You'll have to take the Heathrow flight at ten o'clock. We'll fly you on to Newcastle from there.'

'So what time will we have to leave the ship?'

'Seven o'clock — I'm sorry it's so early. I have the details here.' She held out a sheet of paper.

Leda took it, thanking her, though she didn't feel like it. What a nuisance! It meant she would have no time at all with Nick tomorrow morning.

They finished packing their hand luggage, leaving out their overnight things. Leda had changed into jeans and t-shirt, with a cropped cardigan. When she finally looked at the clock, it was half past eleven. She checked her phone to see if there was a message from Nick . . . nothing.

'I'll put the cases outside, then I'll go upstairs to see if I can find Nick,' she told Ronnie.

'I'm off to bed, dear. It's going to be a very early start, so I want to get some rest. Be careful, now. Remember we have to get away early.'

Leda nodded, but thought she would stay up all night if it meant spending time with Nick!

Although, the way things stood, it didn't look as if he was terribly keen, as he hadn't made any attempt to contact her since the talk. Surely he would have finished in the lounge by now?

Sure enough, when she arrived, the place was empty save for a few people sitting with late night drinks at some of the tables along the sides.

Where could he have gone? She decided on their usual meeting place on the Promenade Deck.

But when she reached it, there was only a group of people drinking and laughing, either sitting at the tables or leaning on the ship's rail. Nick wasn't with them.

The only other place she thought he might be waiting for her was the New Orleans Jazz Bar.

Almost breathless by the time she reached it, she looked in through the door. The lights were colourful, the jazz quartet in full swing, and people were dancing on the floor. But as she surveyed the scene, she could see no sign of him, or Sophie. At least if she found the agent, surely she could tell her where Nick was?

He hadn't told her what time his flight was, but she had assumed it would be later in the day. He had mentioned he had flown from Manchester.

Hesitating, she stood by the door, debating what to do. It looked rather needy, her following him around if he didn't really want to be bothered. She dreaded making a fool of herself.

Then she squared her shoulders. She mustn't be such a wimp! She would confront him in his cabin and find out exactly where she stood. If he wasn't there, she would leave a note, telling him about the new departure time, and it would be up to him if he wanted to contact her.

Still feeling determined, she rapped boldly on Nick's cabin door. She waited, and knocked again, but there was no reply. It was very odd.

Finally admitting defeat, and realising it was now well past midnight, she scribbled a note on a scrap of paper, and slipped it under his door.

Her emotions at rock bottom, she returned to her own cabin.

* * *

After a night of fitful sleep, they were up before six o'clock the next morning. Leda checked her phone again, but there was no message. It was too early to phone him — she would have to wait, maybe even until just before they boarded the plane. She at least wanted to say goodbye.

Ronnie said nothing about Nick, though Leda could see she was curious. The old lady understood that something had gone wrong, and didn't want to make a big thing of it.

* * *

Nick woke with his head throbbing, and cracked an eye open to look at the clock. Eight o'clock! He couldn't remember when he had finally got to bed. In fact, he couldn't remember much of last night at all, after the talk.

Sophie had ushered him off to the noisy and crowded Captain's Bar, where a last night party was in full swing, and he was mobbed by fans. He had promised himself he would only have one drink, and then go find Leda, but somehow the night disappeared into oblivion after Sophie had handed him the drink.

He rolled over with a groan, his head splitting, his mouth gritty and sour. He never usually drank much — how could he have such a hangover?

Overwhelmed with guilt, he pushed himself up to a sitting position. He had wanted to spend a few romantic hours with Leda, knowing they would be going their separate ways today, and he had desperately wanted to know if she would like to continue the relationship.

He would have to go to her cabin and apologise, though how he would explain it, he didn't know. Could someone have spiked his drink? But why?

Suddenly there was loud knocking on his door. Stumbling out of bed, he opened it a crack.

Sophie burst out laughing. 'Look at you! Heavy night?' She pushed open the door and stepped into the cabin. 'You look a bit rough, but after last night, I'm not surprised.'

He shook his head, annoyed at his fuzzy mind.

'I don't know what went on last night, but I certainly didn't intend to drink that much.'

'Don't you remember all your fans buying you drinks? You were too polite to refuse.'

Frowning, he tried to recall it, but failed.

'You'd better get a move on — there's a lot to do before we leave at midday.'

Sophie turned on her heel, dropping her handbag as she did. Quickly she retrieved it and told him she would meet him at eleven o'clock at the information desk for a debriefing before they were due to disembark. She had left the cabin before he thought to ask if she had seen Leda.

After a cool shower and a shave, he opened a bottle of water from the fridge, and drank most of it. Then he dressed hastily in a T-shirt and shorts, thrust his feet into sandals, and loped along the corridor as quickly as he could, down two flights of stairs, and along to Leda's cabin — only to discover the door wide open, the bedlinen in the corridor, and no sign of occupation.

Dismayed and confused, he realised the suitcases would have been taken, and they would had been told to vacate the cabin early because they were leaving at ten. They must be at breakfast.

Taking the stairs two at a time, he reached the dining room and stood at the door, scanning it as quickly as he could. The place was crowded with people, sitting, standing chatting, or carrying plates of food to their tables. He began to walk round, checking every table. Now and then someone would call out to him, 'Hi, Harry', 'Great talk last night'. He acknowledged each greeting with a wave of his hand, but was distracted by his mission.

Having been right round the dining room, he had to admit there was no sign of either Leda or her great aunt. Well, there were so many other places they could be that he decided to phone her. He slipped his hand into his pocket for his phone, and searched through the contacts.

Baffled, he couldn't find any record of her phone number. That was impossible! She had put it in herself — and he had received her text in Barcelona. But the number had vanished — as well as all the records of their texts to each other.

Quickly he checked his other numbers — yes, they all seemed to be there.

It was just Leda's that seemed to have disappeared.

Lost in thought, he almost bumped into someone, and stepped back with an apology on his lips. 'Sophie!' he exclaimed when he recognised her.

'You're miles away, Nick,' she laughed.

'I missed Leda last night. Have you seen her this morning? I know they were due to leave at ten, and for some strange reason I can't seem to find her number in my phone directory.'

Sophie said she hadn't seen her.

'You dropped your phone in the dining room last night, and I saw her fiddling with it — maybe she deleted her number. Remember I gave you your phone before your talk?'

Stabbed with dismay, he exclaimed, 'Surely not! Why would she do that?'

Sophie gave him a look of deep sympathy.

'I don't know, do I? Maybe because she's going home today?'

He turned away, unable to speak for a moment. Had it just all been a

295

light-hearted fling for Leda? He had really thought he could feel her responding to his caresses with genuine feeling. He had had such high hopes, so it was devastating to imagine that she had just been toying with him.

'I'm going to search the ship. Their cabin is vacated, but they must be somewhere.'

★ ★ ★

After a fruitless search around each deck and in every lounge and cafeteria, Nick found himself at the information desk.

There, a large notice caught his eye . . .

Newcastle flight cancelled — ask at information desk for further instructions.

He joined the queue of people waiting, trying not to look too impatient, though he was bursting to find out what was going on.

'The Newcastle passengers were

transferred to the early Heathrow flight, which would be leaving at ten from Palma airport.'

His breath knocked out of him, Nick managed finally to say, 'So when did they leave?'

The girl consulted her sheet. 'Seven o'clock this morning, sir.'

Just remembering to thank her before turning away, his mind was whirling. So Leda had left even before he awoke that morning!

He took out his phone again and scrolled through the missed calls and messages. Nothing at all. Why hadn't she let him know?

He stumbled out into the glorious sunshine, and found a seat at an empty table, where he sat, feeling numb. Of course, he *had* stood her up last night, so she might be angry. But surely she must have deleted her number before the talk? If she had done, that is. Had she planned to disappear all along? He put his head in his hands, confused and despairing.

★ ★ ★

On the bus to the airport, Leda took out her phone and checked it for messages. Still nothing. Should she ring him? He *had* let her down last night, but there could be mitigating circumstances.

She took a deep breath — yes, she would ring, as a final try. It would be pathetic of her just to let their connection from the last few days disappear completely, after her emotions had been stirred to life. Finding his number in her directory, she pressed the green button, and put the phone to her ear. It connected, but rang and rang with no reply, not even an answerphone, so she couldn't even leave a message.

Her spirits sinking, she disconnected her mobile and put it back in her bag.

Ronnie must have realised what she was doing, as she reached out a hand and placed it on Leda's, comfortingly. Leda turned her head a little, and their eyes met. A beam of sympathy came from her great aunt's gaze, and Leda was grateful that she didn't ask questions.

She had no answers. The buoyant mood of the holiday had gone completely.

Leda leaned her head back on the headrest and closed her eyes, blinking back tears and trying to block out the depressing thoughts that cascaded round in her mind.

It was over. Time to move on again. Time to go home to real life.

20

Leda inserted the key in the door of her little house on the outskirts of Newcastle, and pushed it open. She dumped her suitcase in the hall, picking up the neat pile of letters her neighbour had arranged after checking the post each day.

Carrying them through to the kitchen, she turned on the water, opened the blind and filled the kettle. After throwing out junk mail, she had a small pile of letters that needed attention.

Then she checked the answerphone, which was winking insistently. There were only a few messages from some friends, two from suppliers, and lastly one from her mother.

'I'm longing to hear all about it, so ring me as soon as you can,' her mother said.

Leda rested her elbows on the kitchen table and put her chin on her hands.

How much should she tell her mother? She felt such a fool for opening herself up to love again, only to be disappointed. What was wrong with her that she had relationships with disastrous men?

Ronnie had been marvellous, just letting her wallow for a while on the journey home, then cheering her up with reminiscences about their own time together on the cruise.

When she thought back over it, she had been rather prejudiced before the holiday, a little resentful of the fact that she was going to be looking after an old lady. What a revelation Ronnie had turned out to be! Her mind was as sharp as a needle, and though she had been born in a different era and had grown up with different values, she understood how things had changed in the modern world. She had a young attitude, but the wisdom of years.

Leda had grown to love her deeply, and had promised to meet her next week after she had downloaded her photographs on to her computer and printed off a selection for Ronnie.

* * *

Over the next couple of weeks, Leda threw herself into work. She had a new commission starting the week after she arrived home, for which she had to prepare, and she was attending a trade fair at the weekend. It would be a good place to advertise her business, and she had booked a stand several months ago. She had to check her publicity material, and make sure the organisers had all she needed for her display.

Whenever memories of Nick intruded into her mind, she would deliberately make herself think of the places she had experienced without him. She was determined not to brood.

Her meeting with Ronnie was scheduled for the Friday morning before the trade fair. Alhough Leda was looking forward to it, she was apprehensive that it would stir up all the emotions she had rekindled when she met Nick. As it turned out, it was lovely to see her great aunt again as they shared coffee and cake and looked at the photos.

Just before Leda left, Ronnie put out a hand to rest on her great niece's arm.

'Don't be sad about what happened with Nick, dear. It's all part of life. Just a lovely fling.'

'I know, Auntie. I'm doing my best. But he seemed genuine, and I can't believe he ignored us on the last night. He didn't even sign your book!'

Ronnie shrugged. 'That's a small matter. I'm just sorry, and surprised, that he was unkind to you. I expected better. But you must put it behind you. I hear the business is doing well.'

Leda put on a brave smile. 'Work is a good antidote, and I'm certainly busy at the moment. Do you know, I've even had an enquiry from a lady who lives in Sheffield. She's coming up to meet me next weekend.'

'There you are, then! Fancy her coming all this way to consult you. Your fame is spreading. You must make the most of your talents. Someone special will come along, you can be sure of it!'

Leda shook her head. 'No, not for a while. I'm off men. They all seem too wrapped up in their own lives. I'm going to contact my girlfriends and have a big night out in a few weeks, just you see. A good night on the town will work wonders!'

Ronnie laughed as she opened the front door. 'You young people and your clubbing!'

Leda leaned forward and kissed her goodbye. 'You know I'm not wild, Auntie. A few drinks, a good meal, and then some dancing. That's what I call fun.'

'It sounds much like what we used to do when I was young — it just has a different feel, now.'

★ ★ ★

The final preparations for the trade fair kept Leda busy for the rest of the day, and she set off early the next morning to set up her stand, as it was to open at ten.

The day was interesting, and Leda handed out a good deal of publicity material. There were a couple of follow-up enquiries in the week after, so she was able to put some appointments into her diary. In addition, she was busy with her new commission, decorating an extension to a house in the Northumberland countryside.

The week passed quickly and soon it was Friday, the day for her meeting with Mrs Coleman, the woman from Sheffield. She laid out the coffee table, found her best china mugs and a tray, and boiled the kettle, putting a selection of gourmet biscuits on a plate.

Her portfolio was on the large table. She had included a few prints of her latest project, as she was pleased at how well that had gone this week. There were also swatches of fabric and paint colour charts. Satisfied that all was ready, she checked the clock. Mrs Coleman was due any minute. She had told Leda on the phone that she was visiting friends for the day in the area, so they would direct her to Leda's house.

The doorbell rang just before ten o'clock. Leda had no other plans for the morning in case she needed a longer discussion with Mrs Coleman. However, she didn't envisage that it would be more than just an initial talk, as she hadn't seen the property in question. They had agreed that Leda would come and view it if they decided she would take the work.

Leda opened the door to find a tall woman in her late thirties standing on the doorstep. Her brown hair hung in a long bob to her shoulders, and she was dressed in jeans and a patterned blouse with a navy blue jacket on top. The visitor immediately gave her a generous smile, which warmed Leda to her.

She ushered her in, offering her a

coffee immediately. The drinks prepared, she brought in the tray and placed their mugs on the table, then sat on the settee beside her prospective client, who laid down the portfolio through which she had been browsing.

'How did you find out about me?' she asked as they sipped their coffee.

'Someone recommended you. I looked at your website, and liked the designs you had there.' Mrs Coleman chose a chocolate biscuit from the plate Leda offered.

'Was it the Robsons?' This was the couple who had been her last clients before the cruise.

'No, not them. But it doesn't matter who gave the recommendation.' Her eyes flickered away, as if she didn't want to give the name. 'I just liked your designs.'

Leda began to feel slightly suspicious. What was going on here?

'It seems a long way to come for an interior designer. Don't you have any in your area?'

Mrs Coleman laughed and put a hand to her hair, taking a strand in her hand and twisting it.

'Of course, but I don't know any of them. I wanted to see what you have to offer, especially as I was going to be in the area today anyway.' She reached into her capacious handbag and brought out a tablet. 'Would you like me to show you some photos of the extension?'

'Please do.'

They spent the next hour discussing Mrs Coleman's project — a new extension encompassing the kitchen and the living room.

As eleven o'clock approached, her visitor looked at her watch.

'Are you in a hurry to be away?' Leda began to worry her ideas had not impressed the woman.

'Not at all, but I'm getting a lift back, and my driver will be arriving very soon.'

Even as she said this, the doorbell shrilled again. 'I'll get that,' Leda said, putting her notepad and pencil on the seat beside her, then went to answer it.

She opened the door to see a tall man, his back turned to her as he gazed down the street at the view of the hills. For a moment, her heart lurched in half recognition. Surely it couldn't be . . . ?

He turned to face her, and her stomach seemed to do a somersault at the sight of his face.

'Nick!'

He gazed at her for a moment, his eyes filled with kindness.

'Leda — did my sister tell you I'd be coming?'

'Your sister! No, she never said . . . that is . . . well, only that someone would be coming to collect her. How . . . ?'

Her voice trailed away, words failing her.

'How did I find you? Never mind that — it wasn't too hard, as it was. I was desperate to see you face to face and apologise about that last night on the ship. Something strange was going on, and I owe you an explanation.'

'You'd better come in, then.'

Her heart was beating more quickly, but she wasn't sure whether it was happiness or dismay at his sudden appearance. But she needed to hear his explanation and find out why he had let her down at the end of the holiday.

As he entered the sitting room, he greeted his sister. 'Hi, Ella. Had a good morning?'

'Very good, thanks, and I'd like to discuss the project more with Leda, but just now I think I'll go and sit in the car and leave you two to talk.'

The ease between brother and sister was palpable as she took the car keys from him, and flashed a look of compassion between the two of them.

The consultation forgotten, Leda sat on one of the armchairs, not wishing to sit beside Nick on the settee for now. She wanted to look into his face when he was speaking to her, as it would help her judge whether he was telling the truth or spinning a story. All kinds of emotions were warring within her — surprise, delight, anger, offence. She had no idea what to say.

Nick sat in the place vacated by Ella, taking off his jacket and laying it on the arm of the settee beside him. He took a deep breath.

'First of all, I'd like to apologise for leaving you in the lurch after the talk. I do have an excuse, but it probably sounds lame.'

Leda raised her eyebrows for him to continue.

With a sigh, he went on, 'Sophie ushered me off to the Captain's Bar, where some of my fans were drinking. I promised myself I would only stay a short time, but she insisted it was good for publicity. Someone bought me a drink, and I'm sorry to say that the rest of the evening is a blur. My next proper memory is waking in my cabin next morning. I'm not a big drinker, and it wouldn't take a lot to put me out of action. Pathetic, I know, but it's true.'

'Would anyone lace your drink?'

'Well . . . I have my suspicions it was Sophie.'

'Sophie? Your agent?'

'My agent's assistant. My agent is Bella Dubois, and she sent Sophie to look after me for the talk. What she didn't realise was that Sophie had a serious crush on me for some time, and when she saw that I was involved with you, well . . . '

'Oh, come off it, Nick. Not twice — you already told me about your stalker.'

Leda folded her arms scornfully. He must have a very high opinion of himself to think that all these women were throwing themselves at him!

He ran his hand through his hair in exasperation.

'I know, it sounds as if I'm very vain, but it's true. I eventually managed to wheedle out of Sophie that she deleted your number and texts from my phone after you found it in the dining room, and then plied me with drink so I would be unable to meet you. I think she believed that would be enough to break us up.'

'She was right,' Leda said grimly. 'I was furious with you.'

He looked abject.

'I can't apologise enough. I sound completely spineless — and I was. I should have refused to go for that drink and gone straight to meet you. As it was, I tried to find you the next morning, and it was some time before I discovered that you had already left.'

'I left you a note — I slid it under the door of your cabin after midnight. You must have seen it.'

Nick looked bewildered.

'I'm sorry, I never found that. I have no idea when I got back to the cabin, but obviously I was in no state to notice anything. And in the morning . . . ' He stopped and frowned. 'You know, Sophie dropped her handbag when she came wake me up. She must have discovered your note and hidden it.'

Leda still wasn't convinced. She had tried so hard to contact him.

'I phoned you from the bus and you

didn't pick up your phone. I thought you were ignoring me.'

'Sophie actually blocked your number as well, so it never rang at my end. I was beginning to believe that you really had deleted your number as Sophie said, and that you didn't want anything to do with me.' He looked her straight in the eyes. 'But, Leda, it felt so wonderful in your company. I never met anyone who made me feel like that. I couldn't believe you could change so much so quickly. I began to think you'd just been playing with me, having a bit of holiday fun.'

'If I hadn't had to leave early, I would have come to find you. Mind you, I would have probably torn a strip off you for leaving me in the lurch! That really hurt, Nick.'

He leaned over and took her hand in his, pressing her fingers gently.

'I know, I'm sorry. Sophie would have tried to keep you away from me even if you hadn't had to take the earlier flight. It turns out she's a very

314

determined young woman — but now she's a determined young woman working for a different agency. Once we were home, I was so obviously pining for you that she blew up in a temper, saying I was a soft-hearted fool.'

Leda couldn't help laughing in spite of the hurt. 'She actually said that?'

'She did. Then she went on to tell me all the things she'd done, including persuading Bella to send her out to the cruise ship. She didn't mention she'd given her boyfriend the boot a couple of weeks earlier. Her plans were quite elaborate — she just hadn't banked on me meeting an amazing young woman on my first day on the Ocean Star.'

Leda felt her cheeks warm, and turned away. For the sake of her pride, she didn't want to give in to him, but it was so hard to resist. He was masterfully persuasive with his words . . . well, he was an author, after all. Could she trust him?

When she made no reply, Nick continued, 'I'm glad to say my agent was very angry with her. Bella wanted to dismiss her outright, but in the end I persuaded her to find Sophie a position with another agency. These agents are all great buddies, you know, they meet each other regularly at events and awards.' He sighed, long and deep. 'Can you ever forgive me? I'm so sorry I upset you — it was never my intention.'

Not wanting to let herself be won over yet, Leda withdrew her hands from his grasp.

'How did you find me?'

'It wasn't hard. I found your business online. Then I had to work out how to approach you without you slamming the door in my face — as I knew you had every justification to do. I confided in Ella, and she worked out our strategy.'

'So there is no job, it was just a ploy to see me.' Disappointment and annoyance warred in her, as she had thought she would enjoy working with this project — and with Ella.

'Not at all. Ella does have a new

extension, and she does like the idea of an interior designer — although we didn't know if you would want to work with her once you knew who she was.'

Unable to gather her thoughts into anything remotely coherent, Leda stood up and walked over to the window.

'I don't know what to think, Nick. I was getting used to blocking out your memory, and our time together, from my thoughts.'

He came up behind her softly, and slipped his arms round her waist.

'Why did you have to work so hard at forgetting me? Didn't you believe I was too despicable to even consider?'

Almost instinctively, her body melted into his.

'I don't know . . . Oh, because it hurt! I've had enough of being put down, and made to feel worthless! I want someone who's going to value me and cherish me . . . ' Her voice trailed away.

He swung her round to face him.

'Leda, I know we live some distance

apart, but I believe that something special started on that holiday. It wasn't just a fling, was it? At least, it wasn't for me.'

Searching his face for the truth, in the end she believed his words, and nodded.

'It was more than a fling for me, too. I so hoped we would have this conversation before we left the ship. But my dreams turned to dust, and I wonder if it's too late now. I've spent the last few weeks wiping you and any feelings you awakened in me out of my mind.'

Disappointment crossed his features and he dropped his hands from their grasp on her arms.

'It's my own fault, I know. But please don't let us lose this, Leda. Could you begin to build a lasting relationship with me? After all, I'm a writer, and I can write anywhere.'

Leda knew she wanted to say yes, but in the past weeks she had worked hard to build her shell again. Could she let it be cracked so easily?

Then she remembered Ronnie's words . . . *If you cut yourself off from love, you'll have a big hole in your life.*

She raised her eyes and looked deeply into his. Could she really gaze into Nick's soul, and what would she see there? She knew what she wanted to see, and suddenly she let herself relax. Love and happiness flooded her being as she held out her arms.

With a cry of delight, he pulled her to him, crushing his lips against hers. The room seemed to explode around them. A deep, long forgotten sensation of wellbeing filled her as she pressed her body to his, wanting to be enveloped by his love. On and on they kissed, not wanting to break their connection. At last, they drew apart. Leda's eyes were moist with emotion.

'Darling Leda,' was all he said, folding her against him in his arms. As she laid her head head on his shoulder, peace and contentment washed over her.

They stayed like this for several minutes, each savouring the sensation of the other so close, until they finally drew apart and he looked deep into her eyes.

'So when can you come to stay with me? I'd love you to see my cottage — and my dog, Maisie.'

Leda liked the thought of staying with this man and his dog. She longed to see his everyday life, live in his world.

'I can do next weekend, if that's not too soon.'

'It could never be too soon. And I hope it's going to be a regular occurrence.'

'You can stay here, too, of course . . . maybe the following weekend?'

'You bet.'

He hugged her again, kissing her lips briefly. Then his face took on a more sober look.

'I'd better let Ella know what's going on. She'll be on tenterhooks, waiting in the car.'

'Would you both like to stay for

lunch? I can easily rustle up something.'

He sighed. 'Much as I would love to, we have to be going. Ella needs to be home as she's got two boys to pick up from school.'

A picture of Nick as an uncle with a family waiting for him flashed into Leda's mind, and filled her with longing to be a part of it.

Her eyes took on a wild look, and she blurted out, 'Nick, can I come with you, now?'

'Right now?'

For a heart-stopping moment, she thought he would back down, that it was too much too soon. But an instant later his face shone with joy.

'Of course! How soon can you be ready? And how long can you stay?'

'Until Monday,' she breathed. 'Give me two minutes to throw some things in a bag. We'll have to make a brief stop in Durham, if that's all right.'

He looked bewildered. 'Durham?'

Her whole being flooded with warmth.

'There's a special old lady who will be so thrilled to know that you found me. And you still have to sign her copy of your novel!'

Nick's face relaxed into a smile.

'Of course! We can't forget Ronnie. After all, she brought us together. She should write romance novels, not crime!'

Laughing, Leda ran from the room, her whole being filled with hope for the future.